TARNISHED HEROES

To Joyce
with love
from Bryan

Also by Bryan Marlowe

❀

Memoirs of an Errant Youth

As Long as There's Tomorrow…

TARNISHED HEROES

❀

Bryan Marlowe

iUniverse, Inc.
New York Lincoln Shanghai

Tarnished Heroes

Copyright © 2006 by Bryan Marlowe

All rights reserved. No part of this book may be used or reproduced by any means, graphic, electronic, or mechanical, including photocopying, recording, taping or by any information storage retrieval system without the written permission of the publisher except in the case of brief quotations embodied in critical articles and reviews.

iUniverse books may be ordered through booksellers or by contacting:

iUniverse
2021 Pine Lake Road, Suite 100
Lincoln, NE 68512
www.iuniverse.com
1-800-Authors (1-800-288-4677)

This is a work of fiction. All of the characters, names, incidents, organizations and dialogue in this novel are either the products of the author's imagination or are used fictitiously.

ISBN-13: 978-0-595-40750-7 (pbk)
ISBN-13: 978-0-595-85115-7 (ebk)
ISBN-10: 0-595-40750-1 (pbk)
ISBN-10: 0-595-85115-0 (ebk)

Printed in the United States of America

To Kathleen, of course

This thing of being a hero, about the main thing to it is to know when to die.

> —*Will Rogers, Actor, Humorist and Philosopher*
> *(1879–1935)*

Acknowledgements

I thank Charles Muller, my editor and agent, who has given me much encouragement and advice in the writing of this novel.

In the epilogue of this novel I have borrowed two lines of John Henry Newman's hymn:
Lead, kindly light, amid the encircling gloom.

CHAPTER 1

✻

Group Captain Randolph Tremayne, RAF, Her Britannic Majesty's Air Attaché serving in the British Embassy in Bangkok, was an embittered and unhappy man. He had been in his present post for nearly four years and he considered that he had done his level best to satisfy the military intelligence needs of the Ministry of Defence and the Joint Intelligence Committee (JIC). He had put in more flying hours in the course of his intelligence gathering than any of his predecessors. He had made regular liaison flights in his Devon aircraft to Vientiane in Laos and Phnom Penh in Cambodia—his 'other parishes', as he called them. But he was still an acting group captain with, it seemed, little likelihood of attaining substantive rank before he retired. And no chance at all of reaching 'air' rank; a status he considered he deserved, because of his distinguished war record. After all, he did hold the DFC and bar. And contrary to a wide-held belief in World War II, gongs like that didn't come up with the rations.

Tremayne opened his briefcase and took out his RAF black tie. He'd better put it on, he thought, before H E (His Excellency the British Ambassador), or his deputy, the Counsellor, made the usual daily round of the departments in the chancery. The Ambassador was very particular about how the diplomats and support staff dressed. The order of the day was always lounge suits for diplomats who might need to visit, or receive calls from, Thai

Government officials. The support staff, who spent most of the day in their offices, were also expected to be appropriately dressed at all times and for male staff that included the wearing of sober neckwear.

Tremayne was wearing his khaki drill uniform; obligatory garb, when visiting military establishments, or his opposite numbers in other foreign embassies, and he had been invited to attend a meeting with senior officers of the South East Asia Treaty Organization (SEATO), later that morning.

Tremayne took a packet of Rothman cigarettes from his bulging briefcase. It bulged, not as one might expect, with documents and files, but with a bottle of Remy Martin, a silver hip flask, a carton of Rothman king size cigarettes, a hairbrush, a shaving kit, an assortment of expensive toiletries and, in a secret compartment in the base of the briefcase, a camera and two spare rolls of film.

He lit a cigarette, settled back in his swivel chair and pondered over his mounting problems. His extravagance and high living were the cause of most of them. He gambled and usually lost; unbeknown, but suspected, by his long-suffering wife, he philandered with any woman who would accept his advances; he bore the high cost of sending his daughter to a finishing school in Switzerland, and his son to one of Britain's premier public schools. To add to his financial problems, because of his seniority in post, he was Doyen of the Military Attaché Corps. This extraneous duty involved entertaining his Attaché Corps colleagues and members of the Thai Armed Forces.

The closing of the adjoining general office's external door disturbed Tremayne's thoughts. It was his personal assistant, Flight Sergeant Barry Marshall, returning from an early visit to the local bank, to draw cash to cover departmental expenses.

Tremayne straightened up in his chair, extinguished his cigarette and called out in an unnecessarily loud voice, 'Barry, you can bring the mail in now.'

Barry gave a deep sigh and gathered up the mail that had been received in the diplomatic bag in the chancery registry that morning. Holding a 'Top Secret' security clearance level, he was authorised to open all the mail and record the receipt of the classified correspondence. This he had done in readiness for the group captain's summons. He tapped lightly on his door.

'Come in, Barry, come in!' Tremayne almost bawled. 'What have you got for me this morning? Anything worthy of my attention?'

Barry placed the mail on the group captain's desk. 'Not a lot, sir, just a few routine and lowly classified letters from the Directorate of Intelligence; an acknowledgement of your last roll of film; a batch of developed prints, all stamped "secret". I think they're the ones you took of the new airstrip at Sattahip. And, of course, the latest issues of Defence Council Instructions and Record Office Memoranda.'

Tremayne grabbed the packet of photographs and looked through them. 'These are good, very good. The JIC will be pleased; they've been after something like this for weeks. The runway looks almost complete and should be ready for use by the USAF's heaviest bombers in a few weeks. Once the Yanks start operating their long-range heavies from Sattahip, the North Vietnamese Army's Ho Chi Minh Trail into South Vietnam will be in for a real pasting.' Tremayne looked up at Barry with a smug look on his face. 'Leave all the photos with me. I'll pop down to see "The Friends" with these. They'll be delighted with them. You can take the rest of this bumph and deal with it.'

Barry collected up the correspondence and turned to leave the office.

'Hold your horses, Barry; there's a most urgent job I want you to do for me this morning. I want you to cobble up a claim for my monthly entertainment allowance. Make sure it's for the maximum amount. You know the score, a dinner party, or buffet supper, for about a dozen Thai generals and their ladies—that should justify the amount of the claim. If the MoD want worthwhile intelligence reports they can't expect me to skimp on the entertainment of my most reliable sources of information.'

Barry refrained from making any comment. He knew from bitter experience that it was unwise to question the group captain's instructions. He also knew that the group captain would not be spending any money on entertaining Thai generals and their wives. It was more likely for him to take a couple of middle ranking, or even junior, officers to a massage parlour to enjoy something more gratifying than a massage, and then to go on to some sleazy night club, of which Bangkok abounded. There he would get them pissed enough to answer his questions about classified military matters—their answers to which would almost certainly result in them facing a court martial if their superiors found out.

'I'll attend to that matter as soon as I'm can, sir. I've received quite a lot of requests for over flight clearances from Changi this morning. There's five or six Hastings flying up to Leong Nok Tha this week. I'll be glad when the Royal Engineers finish that airfield. It'll certainly reduce the number of aircraft clearances we have to arrange with the Thai Ministry of Foreign Affairs.'

Tremayne gave a little yawn. 'More signals, or rather telegrams, eh?' In spite of his years with the Foreign Service, he couldn't get used to the Foreign Office term "telegrams", when referring to military signals. 'Well, you'd better buzz off and get them done then. I'm off to SEATO Headquarters at eleven. I'll probably stay for their free luncheon, so I'm not likely to get back to the office this afternoon.'

Barry left the group captain and returned to the general office. Roy Hughes, the Naval Attaché's pompous PA, who thought that he, as a Civil Service clerical officer, had the status of a Royal Navy sub-lieutenant and was senior to all non-commissioned officers, and Diana Wright, the Defence and Military Attaché's P.A., a self-adoring corporal acting staff sergeant, were discussing the latest news about the possibility of Sterling being devalued.

Barry didn't join in their conversation, he rarely did; he thought them boring and self-centred—not his kind of people. He sat quietly at his desk, smoking a cigarette and drafting out the aircraft clearances. He knew the group captain wouldn't be back that afternoon. After his protracted luncheon ('You mustn't call it lunch in the Foreign Service,' he would say.) he'd be off to the golf course. He always kept his golf clubs in the boot of his official car. 'You never know when you might get the opportunity of playing a few holes, and golf courses are often the best places to pick up useful intelligence,' was his excuse.

CHAPTER 2

The much-decorated Lieutenant Colonel Bradford Rantzen, USAF, Assistant Air Attaché, employed in the Embassy of the United States of America, in Bangkok, was a worried man. He knew he was failing at his job. He was 52 years old, had been passed over for further promotion because, as he would freely admit, he was past his best. He'd had his day though; as a National Guard pilot he had joined the American Eagle Squadron and fought in the Battle of Britain, shooting down five enemy aircraft, thus qualifying him as an 'ace'.

After the Japanese sneak attack on Pearl Harbour, on December 7, 1941, which brought the United States into the war, Rantzen transferred to the US Army Air Corps. Because of his previous combat experience he was made a squadron commander, with the rank of major. He served with distinction in the South Pacific theatre of operations and raised his tally of enemy kills to fourteen.

At the outbreak of the Korean War, in June 1950, he was promoted lieutenant colonel and given command of an F86-Sabre fighter wing. He again distinguished himself in aerial combat, shooting down three North Korean Migs.

While Rantzen was patrolling south of the Yalu River, with a flight of three aircraft in 1951, a squadron of Migs attacked them. The outnumbering force immediately shot one of his aircraft down. Realising the futility of continuing the engagement against such heavy odds, Rantzen ordered his remaining two pilots to break off and return to base. He stayed behind to cover their retreat. Shooting down one of the Migs and damaging two others, before his aircraft was hit by cannon fire and was set ablaze, forcing him to bail out. He broke an ankle on landing on a rocky slope and was almost immediately captured by patrolling North Korean troops. He remained a prisoner of war in North Korea until he was released, following the United Nations' negotiated armistice in July 1953.

The USAF and CIA intelligence officers, who debriefed Rantzen after his release, noted that he was not very forthcoming about his time in captivity. During the years that followed Rantzen rarely spoke of his experiences in the North Korean prisoner of war camp.

His superior officer, Colonel Harold Merkle, the Defence and Air Attaché, a handsome, charismatic, 39-year-old, high-flying, USAF Academy graduate, and in the frame for a brigadier general's star, had said to him at his recent annual appraisal interview: 'It hurts me grievously to say it Brad, but the fact is you're falling down on the job. It's becoming obvious to everybody that you can no longer cut the mustard. I've covered your ass for as long as I'm going to, and now warn you that one more foul-up from you and you'll be back stateside commanding a recruit-training wing, or military detention barracks, until your retirement.'

Rantzen excused his poor performance at the time, pointing out the emotional pressures he was under: his seriously ill wife, being treated in a hospital in the States; his daughter's recent miscarriage of her baby, which would have been his first grandchild, and his only son, a lieutenant platoon commander with the First Cavalry Division, serving in Vietnam.

A discreet knock on Rantzen's office door brought him back to earth. 'Come in', he called.

Chief Petty Officer Andy Sanders, USN, Colonel Merkle's personal assistant, entered the office carrying several files with red covers. 'Colonel Merkle's compliments, sir,' Sanders said as he placed the files on the desk in front of Rantzen. 'He wants you to represent him at the SEATO meeting this morning. It starts at 11.00 hours, and Colonel Merkle said you'll need to read through these files before you attend the meeting; they contain minutes of previous meetings and the agenda for the meeting this morning.'

Rantzen looked at his watch and groaned. 'Hell's bells, it's 9.20 now! How the fuck am I supposed to read all this crap before I go to the meeting? It's a 20-minute drive to SEATO Headquarters when the traffic is light, and today it looks heavier than usual.'

Sanders put on a sympathetic look. 'Sorry, sir, but the colonel said he has an important meeting with Major General Sawat Prasang, the RTAF Intelligence Chief, which clashes with the SEATO meeting, and instructions from the Pentagon state that all SEATO meetings must be attended by the most senior representative of this department. Unfortunately the Military Attaché is attending a Thai Army jungle warfare exercise up country and the Naval Attaché is attending Vice-Admiral Boon Chanon's funeral. And you *are* the senior assistant attaché. Is there anything I can do to help, sir?'

Rantzen laughed aloud. 'No, but thank you for the thought, Andy; just leave me alone to get on with my reading.'

'Very well, sir,' Sanders said as he turned to leave the office.

'Oh, yes, Andy, there is something you can do for me—book me a staff car from the motor pool and detail the best driver they have available to stand by for my departure.'

Sanders smiled warmly; he, like most of the junior officers and enlisted men employed in the embassy, had great respect for the lieutenant colonel. 'Consider it done, sir.'

Rantzen gave a deep sigh and started to scan the files. *That high-handed son-of-a-bitch is sure making life difficult for me*, thought Rantzen as he quickly turned the pages of the files. *And he can't even tell me straight. He has to send his gofer to give me instructions. One of these days I'll make him wish he'd never treated me like a wet behind the ears, shavetail lieutenant.*

CHAPTER 3

❁

'How did yesterday's SEATO meeting go, Randy?' enquired Colonel Thomas Purvis, the Defence and Military Attaché as he and Tremayne entered the chancery building.

'Not much worth mentioning, Tom, nothing we haven't heard before, just paranoiac chuntering from the Americans; warning us *again* of the communist threat to the stability of South East Asia. They're worried hairless, that if South Vietnam is taken by the Communists, Laos, Cambodia and Thailand will be the next dominos to fall.'

Purvis laughed thinly. 'Their position is, I suppose, understandable. If Thailand did turn red, which I personally think is highly unlikely, the Americans would lose a tremendous amount of prestige in South East Asia, and it would put SEATO on the spot. Could even mean the dissolution of the treaty, or total war for all its members. Of course the Americans must be disappointed that we didn't throw in our lot with them this time, like most of the other SEATO members. But the Prime Minister and the Foreign Secretary have made it quite clear that we'll not get drawn into any more "police" actions against the Russian and Chinese backed Communists. Look at what's happened with Korea, and the military intervention *there* had the full backing and support of the United Nations.'

'I have to agree with you, Tom, but there are times when decisive military action, or hard talk, is needed. It's not just a matter of following Teddy Roosevelt's favoured foreign policy of "speak softly, and carry a big stick". There are times when you have to call your antagonist's bluff. As Kennedy did, with the Russians over the Cuban Missile Crisis.'

'That's enough history for this morning, Randy; all this talking has given me a thirst, as I'm sure it has you. Come into my office and I'll get Diana to make us a cup of coffee.'

Drinking coffee in Tom's office, their conversation turned to more mundane matters.

'I saw Brad Rantzen at the meeting; he went in place of Harold Merkle. He didn't seem with it.'

Purvis raised his eyebrows slightly. 'Well, he's had some personal problems to deal with lately, which must affect his performance. I feel rather sorry for the chap.'

'Yes, Tom, I do, too; he tells me all about his problems every time we meet. But I think he might have prepared himself a little better for the meeting. He seemed all at sea and at a loss for anything worthwhile to contribute to the meeting.'

'Come, come now, Randy, be a bit more charitable, and remember that, like John the Baptist, King Charles I, and General Custer, we all have our *off* days.'

Tremayne laughed out loud. 'Now, after *that one*, Tom, you'll have to excuse me, I must get back to my office. I've reports to write to cover those photos I took of the new runway at Sattahip.'

'OK, Randy, see you later.'

Writing reports was not Tremayne's present top priority. He needed to get his hands on some ready cash quickly. He had an appointment with two Royal Thai Air Force squadron leaders from the northern Thailand RTAF base at Udorn that evening and had promised to take them to his favourite massage parlour on the Patpong Road.

As he passed his assistant's desk in the general office, he tapped Barry on the shoulder and asked in a voice barely audible to Barry, so that the other two assistants in the office wouldn't hear: 'Have you prepared my claim?'

Barry nodded and whispered, 'Yes, sir, shall I bring the cash box to your office?'

Tremayne returned his nod and whispered, 'Straight away, Barry'—and returned to his office.

Barry collected his cash box from the strong room and took it and the prepared claim to Tremayne's office.

'I've made out a claim for your entire monthly allowance in respect of a buffet supper in your home, for the number of guests you gave me. We couldn't call it a dinner party, because your dining table is only large enough for 14 place settings.'

Tremayne grimaced. 'Oh, for Pete's sake don't be so bloody pedantic. Who the devil knows, or cares, about the size of my dining table? Just give me the money!'

'With respect, sir, H.E. does for one; you have had him and Lady Humphrey as guests for dinner on at least one occasion since I've been here.'

'So what! Do you think for one moment that the Ambassador sees, or really cares about, every pettifogging claim made by his senior staff.'

'No, of course not, sir, but all our expenditure is subject to audit by the Ministry of Defence (Air) and a dinner party for a dozen Thai generals and their wives might seem a little bit over the top, even for an officer in your position,' Barry replied, as he opened his cash box and counted out the required amount of Thai bank notes. 'Here you are, sir, two thousand, eight hundred and fifty baht. Please sign your claim form.'

Tremayne took the money without a word, scrawled his signature across the bottom of the claim and pushed it across his desk to Barry.

Barry picked up the form and his cash box. 'Will that be all, sir?'

'Not quite, Barry; before you go back to arranging aircraft over-flight clearances, I want you to collate all the information we have on the RTAF base at Sattahip and make a chronological file of all the papers. I shan't be in tomorrow until about ten o'clock, and as soon as I get in I want to dictate a covering report to accompany those photographs I'm sending to the JIC. My report must be ready to catch the late afternoon bag for London.'

'I'll make it my next job, sir,' said Barry, trying not to grin as he thought about why the group captain would not be in until ten o'clock the following morning.

CHAPTER 4

❀

Tremayne stepped out the shower stall in The Seventh Heaven massage parlour, selected a fluffy white towel from those hanging on a bamboo rail against the wall and started to gently rub his body dry. He had been in the Far East long enough to know that to rub oneself briskly after a shower would cause the body to sweat profusely. Despite the air conditioning in The Seventh Heaven, he had been perspiring excessively for nearly an hour while engaged in coupling with his favourite hostess, 'Nit Noy', as he called her. She certainly knew her onions when it comes to giving a man 'the best sack time he ever had', he thought. He felt completely satiated. All he needed now was a large Remy Martin cognac to complete his feeling of euphoria.

His two companions, Squadron Leaders 'Mutt and Jeff' as he called them, were still humping away in the adjoining cubicles. But then, he was 46 and could give them both a dozen and more years. He looked at himself in the long wall-mounted mirror. Not bad for 46, he thought. He was an inch or two over six-feet tall, proportionately built, with muscular arms and legs. Years of playing golf and squash had helped him maintain his still youthful frame. He had a good head of dark brown hair, greying slightly at the temples, and dark brown eyes, the whites of which were often reddened by his liberal consumption of brandy. *I must remember to get some more of that Grecian stuff*, he thought. His face and body was tanned by hours of reclining on a sun-bed beside the pool in the British Club and on the beaches at Hua Hin and Pattaya. A Cesar Romero type moustache added interest to his regular features.

Squadron Leader Mutt, clad only in boxer shorts, was the first to leave his cubicle. He glanced at Tremayne's naked body, gave a sheepish grin, a sign that he was embarrassed, and hopped into a vacant shower stall.

By the time Squadron Leader Jeff had emerged from his cubicle, Tremayne was clad in tan chinos, a colourful Thai silk shirt and suede loafers.

'Jolly good fuck, thank you, group captain, sir,' he said as he entered the shower stall vacated by Mutt, who was now, like Tremayne, dressing in mufti.

Tremayne gave a wolfish grin. 'I've paid the madam, so look lively, you two; I'll be waiting for you in the car.' Tremayne had given Samarn, his Thai driver, the night off. There was no danger of Samarn reporting his activities to 'Madam' Tremayne, but servants' gossip was passed from one household to another and could quite easily finish up being talked about in the embassy compound.

The two officers came out of the parlour together and got into the back of the roomy saloon.

Tremayne turned to face them. 'Hey, you two, I'm not your flunky driver! One of you come and sit up front with me.'

They both grinned with Thai embarrassment and, in chorus, apologised, 'Sorry, Your Excellency.'

The two officers talked earnestly in Thai for several seconds. *Probably debating about who's senior and should sit next to me*, thought Tremayne. Then Mutt got out of the car and came round to the side of the car and got in beside Tremayne.

Tremayne released the handbrake and slowly drove away from The Seventh Heaven.

'If you two have no particular preference as to where you want to go, I've got a lively little club in mind. It'll probably be full of American troops on leave from Vietnam, but is not frequented by any of your military personnel, and is hardly the place where you might bump into any embassy staff. It's a newly opened place, on Soi Cowboy, between Sois 21 and 23 on Sukhumvit Road.'

'Sounds OK, sir, you seem to know all good places for enjoyment,' Jeff said. 'We're from Chiang Rai but live with our wives and children on RTAF base at Udorn, and rarely come to Bangkok.'

Tremayne laughed. 'All right lads, hold on tight, we're taking off for a rare old night of wine, women and song.' Tremayne grinned as he pressed the accelerator to the floor, sending the car hurtling along the Sukhumvit Road.

Arriving at the club, Tremayne drove the car into the shadows under an overhanging tree. He didn't want the car's CD plates to be seen by anyone who might be curious enough to enter the club to see the owner of the vehicle.

Tremayne led his companions to a table in the corner of the bar, a position from which he could immediately spot people entering and leaving the club. Like that of most of Bangkok's nightclubs, the bar was almost in darkness. The only lighting near the tables was that afforded by candles.

Frank Sinatra was making a pleasant enough sound, singing *Strangers in the Night*, a current hit tune. Well, that's the *song*, thought Tremayne, now for the *wine*. A tiny hostess, apparently young and attractive, at least in candlelight, came to their table.

'What would you rike, sir? You want me get you velly nice cocktail?' she asked, leaning over the table and exposing her petite cleavage to within a few inches of Tremayne's face.

Tremayne laughed, not at the sight of the hostess's straining breasts, but at her pronunciation of the letters 'L' and 'R', a common difficulty for oriental races. It reminded him that his Thai cook would ask him every morning, 'Are you frying today, Master, or shall I make you a flyed blekfast?'

Now we have the *women*, thought Tremayne, as he lightly pinched the inside of the girl's exposed thigh. The girl made no objection, nor did she back away from the table. She'd experienced so much more from the western *farungs,* who were always trying to touch the most private parts of her body. She sensed that this party were good time guys, with money and were probably good tippers. Those she could put up with making their lewd advances. She stood with her pad and pencil poised to take their order.

Tremayne gave a cursory glance at the Singha beer-stained drinks list. 'No cocktails, thank you; make it two large Mekong whiskies for my friends.' That'll be good enough for them; buying them expensive imported Scotch would be like feeding donkeys strawberries, Tremayne reasoned. 'And I'll have a triple Remy Martin.'

'Okey-dokey, good sir,' said the girl as she moved quickly away from the table, but not quick enough to avoid Tremayne's light slap on her rump.

The girl returned with the drinks and placed them on the table, before Frank Sinatra had finished with the nocturnal strangers.

Tremayne tipped the hostess by pushing a five baht note into her cleavage. The girl giggled and tottered away on her ridiculous high-heeled shoes. An image of Minnie Mouse came to his mind as he watched the girl's bottom waggling in her too tight mini-skirt as she returned to the bar.

He took a deep swig from his brandy glass and turned, smiling, to his companions. 'Well, guys, what's new at Udorn? Have your

American allies been making any major raids over North Vietnam, or for that matter, anywhere else? Is the CIA still operating in Laos from there?'

Mutt and Jeff exchanged uneasy, questioning, glances. Mutt, the senior, became spokesman. 'The USAF are bringing in more heavy bombers and have stockpiled ordnance at the base, but then you must surely know that from your conversations with the American military.'

Tremayne nodded. 'Yes, but what about the CIA? Do they operate from that base?'

Mutt took a sip of his whisky before replying. 'Yes, they do. I thought that was common knowledge among SEATO members.'

Tremayne smiled. 'Yes, it is, but our American friends sometimes treat us like mushrooms, so we find it is better to get confirmation of facts from those actually on the ground.'

Mutt looked puzzled. 'Mushrooms?'

'Yes, like mushrooms, we're kept in the dark and fed on bullshit!'

Mutt and Jeff laughed loud enough for several heads to be turned their way from the nearby tables.

Tremayne drained his glass and the two officers quickly followed suit.

'Ready for another drink, gentlemen?' Tremayne asked as he waved his hand in a 'same again' motion to the hostess by the bar. Mutt and Jeff nodded in unison.

'Minnie Mouse,' as Tremayne now thought of her, tottered to their table with the tray of drinks. She stood close to Tremayne, pressing her bare thigh against his arm while she waited for a tip. Tremayne leered at her and pressed a rolled up one-baht note deep into her cleavage. The girl gave a sulky look and moved away. Her experience as a bar hostess had taught her how to distinguish the size and value of notes stuffed between her breasts.

As the evening wore on Tremayne realised he had lost the attention of his now convivial companions and wouldn't get much useful information from them. They were ogling every woman in sight of the table and telling Thai dirty jokes, the punch lines of which were meaningless to Tremayne. He decided a different tack—a personal approach. Most people enjoy talking about themselves. 'You said you were both from Chiang Rai. I've flown over the town several times but I've never landed there. What sort of a town is it?'

'Yes, we're from Chiang Rai,' they answered in chorus. 'It very good town, many interesting buildings.'

Tremayne lit a Rothman and passed the packet to Mutt and Jeff. They both took a cigarette and lit up. Tremayne then questioned them about their wives and children, but slowly steering them back to talk about what was happening in the north of the country and neighbouring Laos.

'Chiang Rai—it's in The Golden Triangle, isn't it? I've heard all sorts of interesting things about what goes on there, from the Air America crews who fly up to Laos.'

'Yes, The Golden Triangle, or as we call it in Thai, *sahm lee-um torng kum*,' answered Jeff. 'Many bad men sell drugs—heroin and opium, made from poppies grown in Laos.'

'Is the Thai Government doing anything about their activities?'

Jeff looked questioningly at Mutt for guidance. Mutt ignored him and answered confidently, 'Oh, yes, certainly, the army and the Thai Border Patrols are very active around Chiang Saen. They kill, or capture many drug dealers.'

Tremayne wasn't learning anything new from the RTAF officers that he hadn't already heard from other sources, but they were *confirming* what he had heard. He didn't know why, but he was becoming interested. 'Who buys all the drugs?'

'Oh, all sorts of peoples, even Americans, Europeans and Australians buy the drugs, to smuggle out of the country. If Thai men buy drugs to sell and get caught they get chop with machine gun,' said Mutt, drawing his right index finger across his throat. 'I think they have same law in Malaysia—drug dealers get hanged.'

Tremayne's glass was empty, as were the glasses of his companions. He was about to wave to Minnie Mouse to fetch another round when a disturbance broke out near the bar. He couldn't quite make out what was happening, but from the shouting and cussing he gathered it was an argument between a Thai barman and a GI, who claimed to have been short-changed, which developed into a fist fight. The soldier was much bigger than the Thai, but seemed to be no match for the barman who felled him with two or three karate chops and a well-aimed kick to the groin area. The soldier's buddies then joined in and attacked the barman. While all this was going on the manager of the club or, more likely, a responsibly minded US officer or NCO, must have phoned for the US Military Police, for suddenly the door burst open and several military policemen rushed into the room and started to restrain the GI's.

'Time for us to leave, I think,' said Tremayne to his companions. 'If we stay here we might get our names taken. It would not matter much to me, because I have diplomatic immunity, but you two might get into trouble with your superiors.'

Mutt and Jeff nodded their agreement and followed Tremayne without hesitation as he made for the exit.

CHAPTER 5

❀

'What's Randy the dandy got lined up for us today, Barry?' asked Chief Technician Joe Swaine, a veteran aircraft fitter serving as the air attaché's crew chief, as he entered the general office.

'Not so loud, Joe,' Barry almost whispered. 'Walls have ears and Randy's got the sight and hearing of a shithouse rat; he—'

Barry was interrupted by Diana's call across the office. 'Mind your language, Barry. You know how much swearing offends me, and Roy doesn't like it either. He says it lowers the tone of the office.'

Barry ignored her and said to Joe, 'See what I have to put up with?'

Joe grinned wryly. 'You have my sympathy, Barry. But what were you going to say about Randy's plans?'

'Oh, yes, before I was interrupted, I was about to say that he is planning to fly to Phnom Penh to visit the embassy for a liaison visit. I think it's just a cover so that he can fly some of his American and Thai friends to Angkor Wat. I was going to ring you and Harry up at the house to let you know, but you coming to the office has saved me a job.'

'Let us know what?' asked Master Navigator Harry Simmons as he joined them in the office.

'Oh, hello, Harry, I was just telling Joe about our leader's plan to fly to Cambodia tomorrow. He told me to let you know that he wanted you to file a flight plan for a flight from Don Muang to Siem Reap tomorrow. He wants to take off at 0600 hours. He said he would be flying on to Phnom Penh late afternoon for a night stop at the embassy and returning here, via Siem Reap, the following morning.'

'Bloody hell! That's pushing it a bit,' said Joe. 'How many passengers has he got?'

'Two, or three, I believe,' Barry replied. 'But you know the boss—he could turn up with half a dozen at the airport.'

'There'd better not be more than five passengers,' said Joe. 'The Devon should not carry more than eight persons, and not heavyweights either. Which means a crew of three and a maximum of five passengers. You're his navigator, Harry, can't you tell him?'

'He knows full well what the aircraft's maximum payload is, Joe.'

The group captain's head suddenly appeared round his office door. 'What's all the noisy discussion about?'

Harry's face flushed. 'Oh, nothing really, sir, we were just discussing the Devon's payload.'

Tremayne gave Harry an angry look. 'Didn't Barry tell you what I wanted you to do?'

'Yes, sir, Joe and I were just about to leave for Don Muang, for me to file a flight plan while Joe does his pre-flight checks and refuels the Devon.'

'Good, then off you go,' said Tremayne.

'Just one thing, sir,' said Joe. 'If there is only going to be two or three passengers, may I take two of the seats out of the aircraft to lighten the load?'

'No, you can't,' Tremayne retorted angrily. 'Leave the seats as they are. I shan't know how many passengers we've got until tomorrow morning. Now buzz off and do what's got to be done.'

Harry and Joe made a hasty exit.

'Yes, and there's something *you* can do before the banks close, Barry. Get me some Cambodian currency—Riels. Get five thousand baht's worth. Use money from the imprest account; I'll replace it later in the week.'

Barry gave an almost soundless tut and went to the strong room to collect his cash box.

CHAPTER 6

❁

Harry and Joe were back in their Embassy rented house on Soi 12, off Sukhumvit Road, after their return from Cambodia, and were busy unpacking their gear and soiled clothing.

'Lek, come in here and collect this lot for washing,' Harry called through the window that looked out onto the yard and the servants' quarters at the rear of the house.

Lek, the wash amah, withdrew her hands from her tub of soapy water, dried them on a shirt awaiting washing, and replied to Harry over her shoulder: 'OK, Master Harry, I come now.'

Lek came into the house muttering, 'Too much washing—need more soap powder.'

'Ask Jang's son to go and buy some; here's ten baht, that should be enough,' said Harry, handing her the note.

Lek grinned broadly, stuffed the note into her overall pocket, picked up the two bundles of clothing and walked out of the room

Barry, who shared the house with Harry and Joe, came out of the downstairs shower room wearing a flamboyant patterned bathrobe and went to the tall refrigerator in the corner of the bar area. 'Can I get you two a drink?' he said, opening the fridge and taking out a can of San Miguel beer.

'You certainly can, Barry,' said Joe, smacking his lips. 'I've got a mouth like the bottom of a parrot's cage.'

Barry laughed. 'I know why; it's because you've been drinking too much of that awful Cambodian beer.'

'You're right about that, Barry,' Harry grinned. 'You know our Joe—he'll drink anything called beer in any language. Make mine a fresh lemon juice please.'

Barry laughed, pouring their drinks. 'How was your trip? Any problems?'

'Well, the flight went without hitch, but our leader was his usual self—showing off to the passengers.'

'Yes, and we had too many of them,' added Joe. 'When we got to the airport we found six people waiting for our grumpy group captain. Luckily some of them weren't very weighty, but I had to sit on the floor at the back of the aircraft.'

Barry raised his eyebrows and turned to Harry. 'Six? Who were they?'

Harry shrugged his shoulders. 'I don't know. Joe took their names for the passenger manifest. Mind you, I can't see the group captain putting that lot into his logbook. Some questions might be asked about that if the book were to be examined.'

Joe took a scrap of paper from his shirt pocket. 'Well, there was Colonel Dacres, the US Military Attaché, and his wife; a Thai Air Vice-Marshal Sawat Prasang and his wife and daughter. His wife was a real smashing looking bird—'

'That'll be the RTAF intelligence chief,' interposed, Barry. 'His wife is a famous Thai film star. Tremayne is always creeping around Sawat for information. He plays golf with him and lets him win to make him more amenable. But I wouldn't mind betting that Tremayne is more interested in Sawat's wife than any of the near-worthless military intelligence he might get from him.'

'Well, that's five, who was the other?'

Joe took a deep swig of his beer and consulted his scrap of paper. 'Another woman. Her name was Ruby Carterton, a very attractive blonde in her thirties; an Australian, I think. Well, she had an Aussie accent. She was making notes all the time, so she might be some sort of reporter. Tremayne seemed rather keen on her. He was overdoing his attention to her while we were on the ground at Siem Reap. And she seemed to be enjoying his attentions.'

'Did you take any photographs during flight?' asked Barry. 'Anything worth sending back to the MoD?'

'No photos of airfields, but apparently the passengers took plenty when they were viewing the temples at Angkor Wat,' said Harry.

'Tremayne told me to take some when we were flying over the site,' said Joe, 'but I don't think our intelligence people would glean much military information from them.'

'No, I very much doubt that they would,' agreed Barry. 'I expect Tremayne just wanted them for his "line-shooting" scrapbooks. Anyone else ready for another beer?' Barry walked back to the refrigerator.

'Need you ask?' replied Joe.

'Nothing for me, Barry. I'm not like Joe; I haven't got hollow legs. I've got to watch my weight. I'm now finding it a bit of a squeeze up front in the Devon. I'll get Jang to make me a pot of tea, and then I'll go up to my room for a nap before dinner. I'm afraid I'm beginning to feel my age; I'll be 49 on my next birthday. Anyway, I need a rest to prepare myself for what lies ahead tonight when you two bring all your bar hostess friends in for another of your boozy late night parties.'

CHAPTER 7

❀

Tremayne sat in his favourite cane armchair, in his nineteenth-century, small hotel-like, Thai house, on Sathorn Road. A large Remy Martin was on his side table, within reach of his right hand and he was reading *The Bangkok Post*. A copy of *The Bangkok World* lay at his feet.

'Well, was your journey *really* necessary, Randolph?' enquired Fiona, his wife, from across the huge, sparsely furnished sitting room.

Tremayne lowered his newspaper and looked towards Fiona. 'My journeys are *always* necessary. Remember, I've told you often enough, the purpose of any diplomat, whatever his role in the service, is to *represent*, *observe* and *report*. To enable me to carry out those functions effectively, it is *most necessary* for me to regularly visit my other "parishes". And, of course, the ambassadors of those countries, for which I am the accredited air attaché, expect me to keep them informed about "air" matters in their region. If I didn't they would soon be complaining to the Foreign Office, who would pass on their complaints to the MoD (Air). Don't forget, Fiona, there's a war going on almost all around us, and whilst British military personnel are not *supposed* to be actively engaged in it, our SEATO allies expect our full co-operation with regard to the exchange of military intelligence.'

Tremayne returned to his newspaper.

'What a load of pompous codswallop!' Fiona almost shrieked. 'You know damn well what I'm talking about! Why was it necessary for you to take an aeroplane full of foreign tourists to Angkor Wat? That must be contrary to Royal Air Force regulations—misuse of RAF air transport, or some such thing.'

'From whom did you obtain that information about my flight?' snarled Tremayne.

'From Mrs Dacres, the US Military Attaché's wife, of course, who else? We neglected wives do get together for coffee mornings and often meet at the Embassy Wives' Clubs. She told me that you took her, and her husband, and a high-ranking Thai officer and his family, and a young Australian journalist, called Ruby. She also said that you seemed *enamoured*—I'm sure that's the word she used—with the young Australian woman.'

Tremayne dropped his newspaper to the floor and stood up, his face flushed with rage. 'Now who's talking codswallop? Mrs "nosey" Dacres's gossip is a complete fiction. Apart from Mrs Dacres, who was only on board in deference to her husband, every passenger I flew to Angkor Wat was, in *some* way, connected with my role as an intelligence gatherer, and that's something I cannot discuss with you. I am, as you well know, subject to the Official Secrets Act. Now, if you don't mind, I'd like to drop the matter and finish reading my newspaper.'

Fiona gave a deep sigh and rose from her chair to go to the kitchen.

Tremayne forced a smile. 'Fiona, dear, how's the dinner coming along?'

'That's why I am going to the kitchen, to find out from Sutep,' said Fiona, with a hint of sarcasm.

'Good, then would you be kind enough to tell one of the girls to bring me in another Remy Martin—a large one!'

'Yes, *Master*,' replied Fiona in a mocking tone.

❋ ❋ ❋

As always, unless they had guests for dinner, the meal was not accompanied with much conversation. But Tremayne, anxious to assuage Fiona's upset over his browbeating, introduced small talk about their children. 'We don't seem to have received much correspondence from the children recently,' said Tremayne, with a note of concern in his voice. 'Have Daphne and Peter been on the phone to you lately?'

'Yes, Randolph, they both have. You know they don't like writing letters. "A waste of time," they say.'

'Well, what news had they for us? How are they getting on with their studies?'

Fiona's eyes narrowed. 'As you rarely talk to them on the telephone, I gave you the gist of their news soon after they called.'

Tremayne smiled thinly. 'I know, dear, but please indulge me and tell me again.'

'Well, Fiona's main topic was how very expensive it is in Switzerland. She said that she couldn't manage on the "paltry"—her word—allowance you make to her and asked that you at least double it. She went on to say that her best friend, whose father is some sort of stockbroker in London, gets four times more than she gets.'

Tremayne sneered. 'Her friend's father is a stockbroker, eh? No wonder he can afford to give his daughter such an extravagant allowance. Stockbrokers are among some of the highest paid people in the country. They get almost as much as the so-called celebrities of film, television and sport! What about Peter, what did he have to say?'

'Oh, not a lot, but he did remind us that he was taking his A-Levels this year and hoped to get good passes in religious studies, biology and art. He, like Daphne, wants a larger allowance. I can appreciate his need for a little more, with inflation creeping up as it is at home.'

'Well, that figures. You always did favour Peter. You've made a proper mother's boy of him. He'd not be considered to have much "commissioning potential" in any of the armed forces. And the subjects he's good at are not likely to be of much use to him in making any worthwhile career. What he needs are good passes in English, mathematics, science and physics, if he is to get into a good university and graduate with a degree that will help him make a good future in industry.'

'I don't like to say it, Randolph, but I do think you are being unkind about Peter. He is a very sensitive boy and entirely unsuited for a military career, but I am sure that he will find success in whatever he feels is right for him.'

'Let's hope he does,' said Tremayne in a conciliatory tone.

'Will you be increasing their allowances?' said Fiona.

'Oh, I suppose so. But they, *and* you, must realize that just because I'm a group captain I'm not rolling in money. I have all manner of financial commitments to meet.'

'Yes, dear, I'm quite sure you have,' said Fiona as she left the table. 'It's a lovely evening outside, so I think I'll have my coffee and port on the terrace. Will you be joining me?'

'No, I've had enough conversation for one evening, and anyway, I have some notes to write up about the military situation in Cambodia.'

※ ※ ※

Alone on the terrace, Fiona thought about her 21 years of marriage to Randolph. Looking back to the beginning it seemed that she had made a good match with a handsome young RAF officer, a war hero, who seemed to be destined to reach the highest level in his chosen career. But here she now was, almost 45; her figure, once described as 'delectable' by Randolph, and admired by men and envied by women, long gone; her face prematurely lined and sallow, her hair dry and lifeless because of too much exposure to tropical sun; living with a man she had come to almost hate. She knew he longer cared for her. Their marriage was a sham. The only thing that kept them together was the fact that he did not have sufficient money to leave her. For she had, after one of his brief affairs with a much younger woman, told him that if he ever left her she would really 'take him to the cleaners', and meant it. Since then, philandered he might have, but always returned and promised that it wouldn't happen again. But now, with that Australian woman, presumably of some means, in his sights, he might think she was worth leaving everything he had to her, retire from the RAF, with a useful pension, and make a new life with the new woman in Australia.

🍁 🍁 🍁

In his den, as he chose to call it, Tremayne emptied what remained of the evening's bottle of Remy Martin into his glass, lit a Rothman and sat back in his chair to think. That Ruby woman really was, as they say, 'worth leaving home for'. Their meeting had been by pure chance. Air Vice Marshal Sawat had introduced Ruby to him, explaining that she was a foreign correspondent based in Thailand, but would be moving to Saigon to write an article about the Australian involvement in the Vietnam War.

Later, at a covert meeting with her, she had told him that she had never been to Cambodia and would love to see and photograph the temples at Angkor Wat. He could think of no better way to make progress with her, but to welcome her aboard

TWA—Teeny Weeny Airlines, as Joe Swaine had named the Devon in one of his convivial moments of humour—for a flight to Siem Reap. He had no qualms about justifying the flight with his overdue need to make an official visit to Phnom Penh.

Tremayne drained his brandy glass and lit his ninth Rothman of the evening. A great pity, he thought, it was too late to get another bottle from the bottom of his wardrobe and, anyway, Fiona would now be in bed asleep, and he had no wish to waken her and have to listen to her complaining for the rest of the night about his excessive drinking habits.

There had to be a way to rid himself of Fiona, but short of murdering her to get his hands on her not inconsiderable investments and insurance money, he could think of no way to finance himself for another life with Ruby. He'd have to sleep on it.

CHAPTER 8

❈

Lieutenant Colonel Bradford Rantzen tapped lightly on Colonel Merkle's door. Merkle had sent him a message via CPO Sanders. 'Will you please go straight away to the colonel's office?' Sanders had said to him. 'He has some urgent information for you.' Nothing more than that, so he had no idea what it was all about. Possibly just another bollocking for something he should, or should not, have done.

'Come in, Brad,' called Merkle, in an uncustomary soft voice.

'You wanted to see me, Harold?' Brad said, unnecessarily.

'Yes, Brad, please sit down. I'm afraid I have some bad news for you.'

That soft voice again—it really must be bad news.

Brad sat in the visitors' armchair. 'Bad news—it's not about my son, is it?'

'No, Brad, it isn't. I'm very sorry to have to tell you, it's about your wife. The Ambassador received a telegram a few minutes ago with the news that your wife died in her sleep in hospital last night. Apparently, a tumour on the brain caused her death. Naturally, the hospital will be sending you a full report in a few days. The Ambassador would have told you himself, but he was receiving a Thai minister at the time.'

Brad's face tightened and the blood drained from his face. 'Oh, dear God, she didn't deserve to be taken so early—she was only

48,' croaked Brad, who was near to tears. 'But she's had so much heartache to contend with lately. What with our daughter losing her baby—it would have been our first grandchild. And the worry of having our boy, Benjamin, serving in Vietnam.'

'Brad, I am terribly sorry about your tragic loss. Please accept my heartfelt sympathy. And if there is anything I, or any of the staff can do, please don't hesitate to ask. Of course, you'll want to get back to the States for some compassionate leave. Take all the time you need. No doubt your son will have been informed by now and will be allowed to take a furlough in the States.'

Brad blew his nose loudly and muttered, 'Thank you, Harold. I'd like to leave tonight, if that can be arranged. My daughter, who hasn't fully recovered from her miscarriage, will need all the family support available. Could a signal be sent to Ben, telling him that I am on my way home and hope to see him there soon?'

'Of course, Brad, I'll see it's done straight away. Now you get back to your apartment. Andy Sanders can drive you there, and make ready for a flight tonight. I'll get Captain Denver to give you a call when your flight has been booked. He can take you to Don Muang.'

Brad pulled himself out of the armchair. 'Thanks, Harold, I'll be back as soon as I can.'

'Goodbye, Brad. I hope all goes well for you and your family back home.'

Brad left the colonel's office, wondering just how much worse his life would now be without his beloved Mavis. He'd been so looking forward to her recovering from her illness and joining him in Bangkok. Life, it seemed, wasn't fair for everyone. Some got more tough breaks than they could ever deserve.

🍁   🍁   🍁

Colonel Purvis called his attaché colleagues and their staff to his office, to tell them of the news of the sudden death of Lieutenant Colonel Rantzen's wife.

'Poor old Brad,' said Commander Edward Lancaster, the Naval Attaché. 'He's really having a bad time. One piece of bad luck following another.'

'He certainly is, Eddie,' agreed Tremayne. 'I understand from Harold Merkle that Brad's already left for the States, and his son Ben has been recalled from Vietnam to go home for his mother's funeral.'

'We must send a floral tribute and sympathy cards,' said Purvis.

Everyone murmured agreement.

Purvis turned to his personal assistant, 'Diana, I'd like you to arrange for International Florists to send our floral tributes. Get Colonel Rantzen's home address and other details about the funeral arrangements, as they become available. Your opposite number at the US Embassy—CPO Andy Sanders, I believe—should be able to find out what you need to know. Barry, you are to provide Diana with any cash she might need from the department's imprest account. Randy, as the Doyen of the Attaché Corps, I imagine you will be holding an extraordinary meeting to convey the news to all our colleagues in the Corps, who may not have already heard, and would wish to send their own tributes.'

'Yes, of course, Tom; as a matter of fact, our monthly luncheon meeting is almost due, so I have brought it forward a few days, and have already dictated a memo to Barry. He will see that it is delivered to all of the embassies tomorrow morning.'

Purvis sighed deeply. 'Good, I can't think of anything else. But if any of you think of anything we may have overlooked, please let me know.'

CHAPTER 9

❀

'Ruby, my dear, where shall we meet for lunch?' asked Tremayne in a quavering voice. His right hand grasped the telephone so tightly that his knuckles whitened. He was besotted with this young Australian woman.

'I'm staying here until I leave for Saigon—that is, unless you have something in mind that might induce me to stay in Bangkok,' Ruby whispered in her seductive voice. 'I purposely picked this hotel because it's so near your embassy. So we might as well have lunch here, Randy.'

'No, not The Nana Hotel, anywhere but that hotel, I'm too well known there; that's where our BOAC agent books our aircrews in, when they are staying in Bangkok. Not only that, but my assistant and my crew spend a lot of time there. They get discounts on their drinks on the strength of the bookings. Make it The Imperial Hotel; it's within walking distance of the Nana. I can meet you there a few minutes after twelve o'clock.'

'OK, Randy, if that's what you want. I'll be there at noon. I just hope the beds are as comfortable there as they are at this hotel.' Ruby laughed and put down the phone before Tremayne could think of an appropriate response.

❋ ❋ ❋

'Barry, I'm off to luncheon. I don't know when I shall be back—probably not at all this afternoon. Hold the fort, and if anyone wants me, tell him or her I've found a new source of useful information, which needs further investigation. Between you and me, I think it could lead to something very worthwhile.'

'That sounds very promising, sir, but one thing before you go—would you let me have that 5,000 baht you borrowed from the imprest account? I need it to balance the account before I submit my monthly return to our parenting unit.'

Tremayne smiled thinly. 'Not now, Barry, I have far more important things to think about than your blasted monthly accounts. Remind me about it next week.'

'Very well, sir, but I just hope we don't get a surprise check of our accounts by someone from the Command Accountant's Branch at HQ FEAF.'

Tremayne sighed deeply. 'Barry, in our business, you have to learn to think on your feet and always be ready for the unexpected to happen. So, if a Command Accounts' auditor comes up from Singapore unexpectedly, it'll be good practice for you to talk your way out of trouble. Now, I must fly, I'm nearly late.' Tremayne glanced at his Rolex.

Barry returned to the general office, wondering why Tremayne was dressed in his Saville Row, lightweight, grey suit and smelled strongly of aftershave lotion.

❋ ❋ ❋

Tremayne entered the almost empty hotel bar and saw Ruby Carterton sitting on a stool at the far end of the bar. She held a cocktail glass in one hand and a cigarette in the other. She looked cool, really cool, wearing a wrinkle-free white cotton dress and white leather sandals. The effect was stunning; it showed off her flawlessly shaped, golden tanned body.

Seated in the next but one stool was a young American airman, his two chevrons indicating that he was an airman second class. He was trying to make time with Ruby.

She hasn't seen me, so I'll watch how she handles the situation, thought Tremayane as he stood behind an ornate pillar in the centre of the bar, where he was able to hear their conversation.

'…now Babe, that's no way to treat a guy on his first furlough since he came to Thailand. I mean no harm, just want to buy you a drink and make small talk with you.' The airman moved to the stool next to Ruby.

Ruby turned to face him. 'Now why don't you run along, you annoying pipsqueak, and exercise your charm on one of the Thai girls hanging around the reception area? They'll welcome your attention. I don't!'

The airman's face flushed and his eyes narrowed. 'Just who do you think you are, you old floozie! You're no better than those girls outside. Only a whore would sit at a bar on her own. So what makes you think you're so special?'

Might be time for me to intervene, thought Tremayne.

Ruby looked appealingly at the barman for support, but he gave an embarrassed laugh and returned to polishing glasses. He'd often seen women, on their own, accosted by servicemen and in his experience they had been on their own for that very purpose.

The airman was encouraged by the barman's indifference and leant nearer Ruby and touched her hand.

There's only one thing for it, thought Ruby, *I'll have to deal with this mongrel pest*. She spun round on her stool until she faced the airman. 'I'll tell you who I think I am, Sonny Jim,' she said cuttingly.

'I'm too much of woman for a half-baked, addle-brained, Romeo like you!' In a quick movement she threw the contents of her glass over the airman.

The airman, his face dripping with Mai Tai cocktail, slipped off his stool and fell flat on the floor. Struggling to his feet, he raised his arm as if to strike Ruby. But he suddenly found that he couldn't move. Someone with a steel-fingered hand was holding his neck in a vice-like grip.

'Why don't you run along while you can, or stay here if you want your legs broken,' snarled Tremayne, as he increased his grip on the airman's neck and clenched his right arm with his other hand.

'OK, all right—you win. Let me go! Just who the hell are you?' croaked the airman as he tried to free himself from Tremayne's grip.

'I'm a group captain in the Royal Air Force—that's equivalent to a "bird" colonel in the United States Air Force, and the young lady you have been abusing is a close friend who is waiting for me to take her to luncheon. Now be a good chap and piss off out of here, before I get really angry with you.' Tremayne spun the airman around and sent him sprawling towards the exit.

The airman scrambled to his feet, turned to Tremayne, came to attention and saluted. 'I sincerely apologise, colonel. I meant no offence to the lady. I just felt lonely and wanted to talk to an attractive woman. Please accept my apology and let me buy you both a drink to make amends.'

Tremayne laughed out loud. 'No thanks, airman, there's no need for that. But there's one thing you should remember when next you have a run-in with an RAF or, for that matter, any British officer. You don't salute them unless you're properly dressed, and you are not; you're not wearing your hat!'

'Sorry, Colonel, I guess I've a lot to learn about your strange British military customs.' With that the airman walked out of the bar.

Tremayne joined Ruby who was laughing. 'My word, you are really something,' she said provocatively, touching his hand as he sat next to her.

'So are you! I thought you handled yourself very well. Now would you like another drink before we have luncheon?'

'Why not, Randolph, or do you prefer to be called Randy?'

'Yes, or anything but Randolph. Fiona is the only person who calls me that.'

'So it's Randy then—Randy by name and randy by nature, I'd guess.'

'I should think any man would feel randy with a girl like you at his side,' Tremayne grinned as he sipped his first Remy Martin of the day.

❦ ❦ ❦

Tremayne and Ruby lie side-by-side, smoking in a sumptuous king size bed, in Room 201 in the Imperial Hotel.

'That was rather presumptuous of you, Randy, booking a room for the day. I'm sure you are well aware no girl likes being taken for granted.'

'I did that when I booked our luncheon. It was done with the best of intentions; I thought you might like to freshen up in privacy after luncheon.'

'I certainly need to freshen up now that you've had your wicked way with me.'

'How was it for you, Ruby?' he grinned cheekily. 'I hope I didn't disappoint you.'

Ruby gave a soft laugh. 'No, Randy, you were just fine; or, perhaps I should say, most satisfying. And how about you?'

Tremayne pushed himself up on one elbow and gazed down at Ruby. 'You were wonderful; I cannot remember ever having experienced as much pleasure as you gave me this afternoon.'

Ruby laughed and made to get out of bed.

'No, Ruby, darling, stay a while. You've nothing to this afternoon and I'm not expected back at the embassy. Let's enjoy this time together. Anyway, I'd like to get to know you better. Tell me something about yourself. All I know is that you are a journalist preparing a feature about your country's involvement in Vietnam.'

Ruby smiled as she stretched languidly. 'Well, I'm 34; unmarried and have never had any serious relationships with men, or women. I was educated in Sydney University. Took degrees in oriental languages and media studies. My mother died when I was 13 years of age and I was brought up by my father, with the help of his sister, whose husband was killed in the Korean War. My father is the owner and publisher of *The Sydney Star*. He hopes that I will succeed him when he retires or, more likely, dies, because he's a real workaholic and fully committed to the paper, and I can't see him ever letting go of the reins. He's been sending me on assignments like this one since I left university. I enjoy them and have learnt a lot about looking after myself in tricky situations, and believe me, I've been in plenty of those.'

'Yes, I gathered that, by the way you put that airman in his place. I didn't really need to intervene, but he did look as though he was about to strike you and that's something I could never tolerate—a man using physical violence against a woman.'

'Well, you are what I have been brought up to expect from RAF officers, a perfect gentleman, who knows how to treat a lady. Which is something I've not had too much experience of at home.

But now, sir, what about letting me know something about your life and plans for the future.'

Tremayne put two cigarettes in his mouth, lit them with his lighter and passed one to Ruby.

Ruby laughed. 'I saw that film as well. *Now, Voyager*, wasn't it, when Paul Henreid lit two cigarettes and gave one to Bette Davis? I do believe you are a bit of an old romantic, Randy.'

'Yes, that was the film. But not so much of the *old*, I'm only 44,' Tremayne lied, knocking two years off his age. '*Now, Voyager*, though—I never did quite understand what that title was all about. From some sort of quotation, I suppose.'

Ruby raised her eyebrows. 'You do surprise me, Randy. I'd have thought you would be well versed in the work of Walt Whitman. Actually it's a part of one of his pieces: "The untold want, by life and land ne'er granted, now, voyager, sail thou forth to seek and find"—or something like that.' She gave a little laugh.

Tremayne's face flushed with embarrassment. 'Well, I did drop out of a red brick university at 19 to join the RAF. So I expect my education is a little lacking.'

'That was a great pity. Couldn't you have gone back to university after the war?'

'I suppose I could have, but didn't see the point. When the war ended I was a squadron leader, was newly married, and hadn't any ambitions for a career outside the service, so I decided to stay in and was accepted for a permanent commission. Unfortunately, for one reason or another, you know how plans can go awry in life; things didn't turn out quite as I had hoped and my progress in the service since that time has not been exactly meteoric.'

Ruby looked sympathetic. 'I'm sorry to hear that, Randy. Would it be true to say then, that after serving your country so well during the war, you feel you were rather shabbily treated?'

A chance for me to exploit the situation, thought Tremayne. 'Yes, I suppose you could say that. After all, I do hold the DFC and bar and a couple of mentions in dispatches, which should count for something.'

'Were you a pilot in the Battle of Britain, then?'

'No, I was always in Transport Command, but I did have some hairy experiences.'

'Oh, really, do tell me about them! My father was a lieutenant colonel in the war; he commanded an infantry battalion and fought against the Japanese in New Guinea. He was awarded the military cross for an act of bravery, but never told me exactly what it was he'd done to receive such a high award. In fact, he rarely talks about the war, but still gets dreadful nightmares.'

'Yes, I'm sure that fighting the Japanese in the jungles of New Guinea must have been a nightmare. My experiences pale by comparison.'

Ruby gave a little frown. 'Oh, Randy, don't be so modest, it doesn't suit you. I really am interested in your wartime experiences—so tell me.'

'All right then, sit back and listen if you must. I think my worst moment was when Messerschsmidts shot up my aircraft, a Dakota, and I had to make a forced landing, with the aircraft on fire and one engine knocked out. I got the old kite down and none of my crew were killed or seriously injured. On another occasion, when I was delivering stores and ammunition to our troops in forward positions in North Africa, I was hit by ground fire and the aircraft was virtually inoperable. Because of the danger of onboard explosions from the ammunition, I ordered my crew to bail out and successfully landed the crippled aircraft on my own, without loss of any of the much needed cargo.' Tremayne was beginning to warm to relating his wartime feats. 'There were several other incidents, which drew high praise or awards: Dropping supplies to our airborne troops at Arnhem; flying out casualties from forward positions and under heavy fire from enemy ground forces. I could go on, but don't want to bore you with all my war stories.'

'On the contrary, I don't find them boring; I'm just amazed how you managed to survive the war. But as much as I would like to hear more, I think I ought to be getting back to my hotel. You can phone me there next time you want to arrange a meeting. I shall be interviewing some of the Australian and American officers at SEATO Headquarters to get some background information about the situation in Vietnam, before I go on to Saigon, in about three weeks time,'

'OK, my dear, shall we now share a shower before we part, but soon, I hope, to meet again?' Tremayne said as he swung his long legs over the side of the bed.

Ruby gave a soft laugh as she climbed out of bed and walked seductively to the en suite shower room. 'I'm certainly game if you are, Randy, but with you being so tall, it might be a bit of a knee-trembler for you.'

CHAPTER 10

❀

'Barry, come in, please,' called Tremayne from his office.

I wonder what he wants now? Might be an opportunity for me to get that 5,000 baht he owes the imprest account, thought Barry as he entered Tremayne's office.

Tremayne looked up from his desk as Barry entered. 'Anything in the mail this morning that you can't deal with, Barry?'

'No, there's nothing requiring your attention, sir. It's mainly routine administrative and accounting matters and, of course, lots of aircraft over-flight clearances for flights to Leong Nok Tha. The Royal Engineers seem to be going all out to get the airfield completed before the rainy season starts.'

Tremayne nodded, fingering his moustache—a habit he had when bored, or uninterested in what was being said.

'Barry, where are Harry and Joe? I need them in a hurry.'

Barry looked thoughtful. 'I can only think that they are either at the house, or at the airport.'

Tremayne suddenly looked more peevish than usual. 'Barry, I've told you often enough, keep a track of their movements, so that you always know exactly where they are. Anyway, wherever they are, find them and tell them I want the Devon fuelled up and Harry to submit a flight plan for a flight to Songkhla. Taking off at 0700 hours tomorrow. Oh, yes, and tell Joe that there will only be two passengers. Colonel McMurchy, the Australian Defence Attaché and a woman.'

'Would that be Colonel McMurchy's wife, sir?'

'No, it wouldn't be, and it's nobody's business but mine. Now get on with finding my elusive crew.'

Barry paused at the door. 'Can you now let me have the 5000 baht for—?'

'Not now, Barry,' interrupted Tremayne with growing irascibility.

Barry located Harry and Joe; they were at the house. Harry answered the phone and Barry passed on the group captain's instructions.

'What the hell does he want to go to Songkhla for?' asked Harry. 'I shouldn't think there's anything down there that would be of interest to the MoD (Air). It's a rather exclusive coastal holiday resort near the Malay border.'

'I've no idea, Harry. He wouldn't even tell me who the woman passenger was. I suppose it could be his wife. Frankly, I couldn't care less. At least if he's down at Songkhla, he'll be out of my hair for a day or two. Anyway, can I tell him that you will have everything under control for a 0700 hours takeoff tomorrow?'

'Yes, of course, no problem, Barry, but what about the return flight?'

'He never mentioned anything about that. He'll probably tell you about ten minutes before he wants to return,' Barry said with a laugh.

'That man's impossible!' Harry slammed the phone down.

🍁   🍁   🍁

Ruby Carterton, dressed in khaki slacks, a figure-revealing bush jacket, desert boots and a Tilly hat, was sitting in the near empty departure lounge, talking to Colonel McMurchy, when

Tremayne's Thai driver stopped the official Humber at the entrance door. Ruby looked up and saw the casually dressed Tremayne get out of the car, carrying a large holdall.

'Samarn, I shall telephone Master Barry and tell him when I am to be picked up from here. He'll get in touch with you at the house. It'll probably be about two or three days from now.'

Samarn gave a nod of understanding and drove off.

'Tremayne entered the lounge and walked across to Ruby and McMurchy. 'Hello, Miss Carterton, I'm glad to see you made it to the airport OK.' *Well, one of us is on official business*, he thought when he shook hands with the uniform attired McMurchy.

'Yes,' replied Ruby, 'it was easy. Colonel McMurchy was kind enough to offer me a lift when I told him I was interested in his briefing to SEATO members about the Communist insurgent activity along the Thai Malay frontier and wanted to do a piece for *The Sydney Star*.'

Tremayne gave her a sly wink. 'I don't think we'll see many Communist insurgents. We British got rid of them, one way or another, during the "Malayan Emergency", in the 1940s and 1950s. Those that remained after Malaya got its independence in 1957 are now nothing much more than bandits who raid both sides of the frontier.' Turning to the tall, lean, sandy-haired, and leathery faced McMurchy, he said, 'Wouldn't you agree, Barney?'

'Not entirely, Randy; those that remain may no longer have a cause to fight for independence, but there are very many bandits, as you call them, still hiding out in the thick Thai jungle along the border, and their continuing presence is a major worry for both the Thai and Malayan Governments. That's why I asked you to give me a lift down here. I was a company commander and jungle warfare instructor during the emergency and took part in the training of British and Anzac troops. So the Thai authorities have asked me to pass on my expertise to their local commanders.'

'Oh, I see,' said Tremayne, twisting the ends of his moustache. 'Well, I imagine my crew will have the Devon ready for us to emplane, so shall we trot over to the hardstanding?'

McMurchy and Ruby picked up their holdalls to follow Tremayne.

'Do you need any help with that bag, Miss Carterton,' asked Tremayne with a wicked grin.

Ruby laughed. 'No, thank you, group captain, we Aussie girls aren't used to the pampering your womenfolk get.'

Harry and Joe, dressed in the accepted fashion of chinos and loose fitting Thai cotton shirts, were standing by the aircraft door when Tremayne and his party arrived.

Harry stepped forward. 'Everything is ready for takeoff, sir.'

'Splendid,' said Tremayne, looking at his Rolex. 'It's 0655 hours, so let's climb aboard. Joe, help our passengers to get comfortably seated, and stow all the baggage.'

Five minutes later, after flight checks and clearance from the air traffic control tower, Tremayne took off to fly due south to Songkhla.

CHAPTER 11

❖

'I suppose, with the group captain away for a few days, Barry, you'll be footloose and fancy-free!' shrilled acting Staff Sergeant Diana Wright from her corner of the office.

Silly bitch, what does she know about anything! Barry thought, turning a scowl into a weak smile to answer, 'Hardly, as far as my work goes, whether he's here or away, it makes little difference to me. I still have plenty to do. But it's all the questions I'm asked about his whereabouts, often unknown to me, that waste so much of my time.'

Diana didn't take the hint. 'Well, where is he, then? I've been hearing all sorts of rumours about his carryings-on with women, young enough to be his daughters, and his reckless gambling. You must know he's the talk of the embassy.'

Barry gave a deep and audible sigh. 'Frankly, Diana, I couldn't say for sure, and I couldn't care less either. He did say he was flying to Songkhla. But knowing him he could, at this moment, be canoeing up the bloody Orinoco, or climbing the flipping north face of the Eiger!'

'Language, Barry, remember your language; we are privileged to be working in an embassy and should always conduct ourselves with due decorum.'

Barry muttered, 'bollocks', under his breath and returned to drafting his aircraft over-flight clearances.

Thank God, thought Barry, that sanctimonious twit, Roy Hughes, and the naval attaché were down at Klong Toey to meet the arrival of HMS *Salisbury*. Hughes would have been bound to put his twopenn'orth in to knock Tremayne. Hughes had served a short engagement in the RAF as a fitter on a marine craft unit and would, at every opportunity, broadcast to all who would listen, how much he hated all RAF Officers *and* NCOs, because of the way he had been treated by them.

The office quiet was disturbed by Barry's telephone. Barry picked it up with a silent curse. 'Oh, Mrs Tremayne, good morning.'

'Barry, it *is* Barry, isn't it?'

'Yes, ma'am, 'tis Barry, what can I do for you?'

'Do you know anything about—?'

'Just a moment, ma'am,' Barry interrupted, seeing Diana look up with rapt attention, 'let me transfer your call to the group captain's office.'

Barry switched the call through to Tremayne's telephone, went into his office and closed the door. 'Now, Mrs Tremayne, we are speaking in private.'

'Oh, is that necessary? I only wanted to know when the group captain was going to return from wherever he went. Or, are his movements now classified: "top secret" and for "your eyes only"?'

'No, of course not, Mrs Tremayne, it was just that I thought you wouldn't want anyone else listening in to our conversation. Diana was in the office with me and, I'm afraid, she is a bit of a gossip purveyor.'

'Really, Barry, and what gossip has she to purvey about the group captain—my husband?'

Barry sensed that his efforts to protect the privacy of his group captain's cavalier behaviour were making things far worse. 'Well, all I know is that the group captain flew down to Songkhla two days ago. He didn't tell me, or even his navigator, when they were to return.'

'Songkhla! Why on earth did he go down there? Who went with him?'

'Oh, the usual crew, ma'am—Master Navigator Harry Simmons and Chief Technician Joe Swaine, the engineer.'

'Oh, Barry, don't be so evasive! You know very well what I mean. Who were the passengers he took with him?'

'Passengers? Oh, yes, just Colonel McMurchy, the Australian Defence Attaché, I think the group captain was giving the colonel a lift down to the Malay border to investigate reports about Communist insurgent activities in the area, and one other passenger—a woman. I thought it was you.'

'A woman, and you thought it was me! He never takes me on any of his flights. He says that would be "against RAF regulations". So who was the woman?'

'Well, as it wasn't you it could have been Mrs McMurchy. The group captain was a bit evasive when I asked him who the female passenger was.' It was getting worse and worse.

'Now look here, Barry, knowing the McMurchys, as I do, I am well aware that Nora McMurchy hates flying and wouldn't get into Randolph's Dinky toy aeroplane for all the tea in China! Do you think it could have been that young Australian woman journalist, who's been swanning around the embassy and telling everybody that she is on a special assignment to write articles about the Australian Army's involvement in the Vietnam War?'

Now what do I say? Oh, I know, thought Barry. 'Well, yes, I suppose it could be. That would make sense. She could be on a fact-finding mission with Colonel McMurchy.'

'Hmm,' murmured Mrs Tremayne. 'All I have to say to you, Barry, is that the group captain is very lucky to have such a discreet personal assistant. Goodbye, and thank you for your most useful *intelligence*—I think that is the word the group captain would use.'

'Goodbye…er…Mrs Tremayne. I'll ring you, if I hear any news about the group captain's return.'

Barry put down the phone, sticky with the sweat from his hand. Cripes, he thought, the group captain will be straight in the dogbox when he gets home and no doubt he'd blame him. But what was he to say?

CHAPTER 12

❀

'A penny for them, Randy,' offered Ruby.

It was their third day in Songkhla. Ruby's days had been spent with Colonel McMurchy, who had been lecturing Royal Thai Army junior officers and senior NCOs in the art of jungle warfare, while she made notes and interviewed the soldiers about the situation prevailing along the border. Tremayne had spent his days alone—sunbathing on the golden, sun-drenched beach, thinking, smoking and drinking, but not too much, so as not to weaken his ardour for Ruby. Harry and Joe had spent their time working on the Devon, exploring the idyllic resort and making friends and chatting with the locals, or reading on the balcony of their hotel room.

At night Ruby had gone to Tremayne's room and they had made passionate love. Afterwards they would shower together, lathering each other with exotic soaps and oils before sitting out on the unlit balcony, dressed only in flimsy cotton robes and speak in near whispers about their hoped for plans for the future.

'Oh, nothing much, really, sweetheart,' Tremayne said, grabbing Ruby's hand and pulling her down on his lap. 'I was just thinking that I shall have to return to Bangkok tomorrow. The bane of my life will be conjuring up all sorts of scenarios about what I am doing in Songkhla. I'm rarely away for more than two days, so her imagination will be running amok. I'd like you to return with me so that I can continue to see you before you leave for Saigon. We won't be able to get together much at night but I can come to your hotel in the afternoons. Of course, if you want to stay with Barney McMurchy to finish your article, I'd quite understand. He proposes staying for three or four more days and then returning to Bangkok by rail. A pleasant enough journey, which I'm sure you would enjoy.'

'Randy, darling, you must do what you have to do. Of course I'll return with you. I want to spend all the time I can with you before I leave for Saigon. Anyway, I've done all I need to do with the article. McMurchy's lectures are becoming boringly repetitive, and I've interviewed enough Thai soldiers to get the general picture of what's going on down here.'

'That's splendid, darling, couldn't be better—I had hoped that would be your answer. I'll get the crew to jack up things for our flight back tomorrow. But before we go back I'd like to take you out to the best restaurant in Songkhla, and afterwards to a casino the hotel manager has told me about. We could have a little flutter at the tables before we return for our last night in Songkhla.'

'Oh, do you like to gamble, Randy? I didn't know. But that sounds a nice way to end our evening. My father and I often go to the races at home. We both enjoy the scene and as it happens we're quite lucky. So if you have a flutter tonight, perhaps I shall bring you good luck.'

'That *would* be nice—it's something I sorely need. I haven't had much come my way for a very long time.'

'Never mind, darling, perhaps I can change all that for you. Now I must give Barney McMurchy a ring and tell him that I shall be leaving tomorrow.' Ruby got up from Tremayne's lap and moved to the telephone table.

'No, Ruby, don't ring from this room,' cried Tremayne, a trace of panic in his voice. 'You will have to ask the operator for his number and it will then be known that you have been in my room. And that could take some explaining if it were to be found out by the wrong people.'

Ruby laughed out loud. 'My oath, Randy, you British diplomats are paranoid; it must be that military spy training you get. The telephone operator is hardly likely to be a member of the KGB, or any other secret service. And men having women in their hotel rooms is not likely to be much of a tea-break topic for the Thais who, from what I've heard and witnessed since I came to this country, are well aware and don't much care about the immorality of western *farungs*.'

'I'm sorry, Ruby, for being an alarmist. But you must realise that I need to be careful to ensure nothing gets back to Fiona. She's capable of being very vindictive, and if any scandal attaches itself to me in my present position, and is made known to the Ministry of Defence, via the Foreign Office, I could be sent home in near disgrace; and that would, of course, have a very detrimental affect on my career.'

Ruby looked sympathetic. '*Mai penh lai*, Randy, it doesn't matter, I can leave the call until I return to my room.'

'You haven't taken long to pick up that commonly used Thai phrase. It's as commonplace here, as "I couldn't care less" is in Blighty,' said Tremayne, his worried look now replaced with a broad grin.

'Don't forget, Randy, I did major in oriental languages. But with regard to your now well-hackneyed phrase, the Kiwis have rehashed it to suit their thinking: "I couldn't care less if the cow calves or breaks its leg"!'

They both laughed and Tremayne pulled Ruby to him and kissed her passionately, until Ruby, breathless, broke away from his strong embrace.

'Enough, you sexy beast, save some of that passion for later. What you need to tell me now, is when and where do you want to meet me this evening?'

Tremayne looked thoughtful. 'Let's say 1900 hours, or rather 7 p.m., under those low hanging trees at the side of the hotel. There is much less chance of us being seen there by McMurchy, or my crew. The restaurant we are going to is only five minutes walk from here and I have booked a corner table out of sight of the door. The casino is conveniently next door to the restaurant.'

'That sounds fine. You seem to have got everything nicely arranged for the evening.'

'Yes, my darling, it's what we in the RAF call "forward planning".'

🍁 🍁 🍁

'Did you enjoy the meal, Ruby? I know that Thai food is an acquired taste for most people. I didn't like it very much when I first came out here, but rarely eat anything else now. It's one way to keep the household food bills down,' said Tremayne with a forced laugh.

'Yes, I did enjoy it very much. I've tried most oriental foods—I've had to. In some of the places I have stayed it's been impossible to get anything but the local dishes. I do miss my lamb chops when I'm away, though.'

'Splendid, I'm glad you enjoy Thai food. I foresee Thai food becoming as popular as Chinese food in Europe. My opposite number in the Thai Embassy in London tells me that the first Thai restaurant has been opened in Kensington. I, or rather we, must go there if we ever find ourselves together in London.'

Ruby smiled with her twinkling blue eyes. 'One never knows what the future may hold. Shall we let fate decide our destiny?'

Tremayne reached across the table and clasped her right hand in his. 'Perhaps we can give fate a little help in bringing us together, *forever*. I do love you Ruby and these last few days we have spent together have convinced me that we are well-suited and could have a wonderful future as man and wife.'

Ruby gazed steadily into Tremayne's dark brown eyes, as if trying to read his mind. 'Yes, I have to say, I think I am falling in love with you, Randy, but please, don't rush things. If I came to you, it would be without baggage. But you have a wife and two children, who still need your financial support. You have to consider them.'

'No, that is not the case. Fiona is the one with all the money. She is a wealthy woman and the children are young adults. They will both be in university soon and quite independent of me. Their mother would always ensure that they were well provided for. But enough of all this, let's finish our drinks. I'll settle the bill and then we can go next door and see if we can win enough to pay for our supper.' Tremayne ended his response with a laugh.

'Put your wallet back, Randy. I thought it should be my shout for the dinner. You've paid for everything up to now. I'm not a poor struggling journalist. I don't have to depend on my father for financial assistance. My mother left me comfortably well off. She left me shares, annuities, endowments and a large four-bedroom apartment overlooking Sydney Bay, which I have temporarily leased to one of my father's senior executives. So, you see, I'm pretty well fixed and I have *always* been one to pay my way in any company.'

Tremayne smiled warmly and beckoned the headwaiter to their table. 'Then, my dear, don't let me be the one to break your long held tradition of paying your way.'

❋   ❋   ❋

Tremayne and Ruby entered the casino and were met by a fat, smiling Chinese with a long drooping black moustache. He was dressed in a black Thai silk tuxedo.

'Good evening, sir, good evening madam, I am Wun Cheung, the owner and manager of this establishment and am delighted to welcome you to the Lucky Chance Casino. What is your pleasure? We have roulette, *chemin de fer, vingt* et *un*, craps and poker—stud or draw.'

Tremayne acknowledged him with a nod and Ruby treated him to one of her seductively fetching smiles.

Looks like Charlie Chan, thought Tremayne. 'We'll let you know later. What we would like first is a drink.'

The Cheung looked embarrassed. 'Of course, honourable sir, please follow me and I'll get you a table near the bar.' He led them to a corner table near the end of the bar and beckoned a waiter, another Chinese, to take their order.

'What would you like, Ruby?'

Ruby considered for a moment. 'A champagne cocktail, please.'

Tremayne smiled. 'One of my favourite drinks, I think I'll have the same.' Turning to the waiter: 'Make sure that the champagne is well chilled.'

'Certainly, sir, I understand. We always keep it at the right temperature for drinking.'

While they were waiting for their drinks, Tremayne lit two Rothmans and passed one to Ruby.

Ruby laughed. 'I shall have to start calling you Paul if you continue lighting my cigarettes like that.'

Tremayne looked puzzled. 'Why Paul?

'Paul Henreid, of course!'

'Oh, him! I could never think of you as Bette Davis. You are far more attractive than her.'

'Flattery will get you everywhere, keep it coming,' Ruby laughed.

While they were talking Tremayne had been unnoticeably reconnoitring the customers with a well-trained eye for detail. He noted that they were mostly Chinese gamblers; a few well-heeled, middle-aged Thai businessmen with their too young mistresses, and, surprisingly, so far from Bangkok, a handful of GI's, on rest and recreation leave from Vietnam, accompanied by their 'five-day wives'.

'Randy, I know all about poker, and often have a flutter on the roulette table; but tell me what are the games *vingt et un* and *chemin de fer*? I know they must be French, but what would you call them in English?'

'Well, my dear, *vingt et un*, which I'm sure you are aware, means, "twenty-one", is the French name for what the Americans would call "Blackjack", and what Britons and Aussies call "Pontoon". *Chemin de fer* is a form of Baccarat, or bacarra, as the French call it. The game is a *bete noire* of mine. I lost my shirt playing it one night in Monte Carlo, so I'd rather not talk about it, or encourage you to play it. If you do decide to play the game, the dealer will explain the rules to you. Now I see you have finished your drink. Shall we have another before we chance our luck at one of the tables?'

Ruby's eyes sparkled. 'You can bet London to a brick on that one, Randy, I feel like pushing the boat out tonight!'

Tremayne gave his well practised 'same again' wave at the nearest waiter, who brought their drinks within a minute.

'Shall we make a start with the roulette?' said Tremayne, picking up their glasses. 'I see we have to buy our chips at the tables.'

'Yes, there doesn't seem to be a cash office in sight. I wonder if they'll change travellers' cheques at the tables?'

'I'm sure they will,' said Tremayne. 'But, I see it's an American wheel. I'd rather have had a European one.'

'It's the same as I've played on in Australia. What's the difference?'

'The difference is that the European wheel only has a single zero pocket, whereas this American table has a single pocket and a double-zero pocket which gives the house an advantage of 5.3%, as against that on a European board of 2.7% favouring the house.

'Strike me handsome!' exclaimed Ruby. 'When it comes to gambling you certainly seem to know how many beans make five.'

Tremayne laughed. 'It comes with practise, Ruby. Now let's buy some chips and get on with the game.'

The croupier halted play to change Ruby's cheque for chips. Tremayne noted, with surprise, the amount—US$500, worth about 11,000 baht. Ruby asked for 500 baht chips.

That's equivalent to about £10 each—she's pretty sure of herself, thought Tremayne. He bought ten 500 baht chips, which left him with just enough to pay the hotel bill.

The croupier resumed play. Tremayne placed a chip on Even, one on Black and one on 26—the number of a squadron he had once commanded. Ruby placed two chips on numbers 19-36 and two chips on Even.

The croupier spun the wheel and sent the ball in the opposite direction. It rattled as it bounced up and down for about 20 seconds, then as the wheel slowed down to a stop, the ball landed in a pocket with a plop. Tremayne eagerly craned forward to look at the wheel, but other players obscured his vision. 'Black 26,' called the croupier. He then raked in the losing bets and pushed Tremayne's and Ruby's winnings toward them.

Ruby gave a little whoop as she added them to her pile.

Tremayne quickly calculated what he had won—19,000 baht. This might be the night when he recovered all he'd lost in the past year, he thought joyfully. Ruby must be changing his luck, he thought, as he made new stacks with his pile of chips.

For his next bet, Tremayne pondered for a few seconds, then placed 10 chips on Red, another 10 chips on Odd, and five on 7, the number he always thought of as his lucky one. Ruby randomly tossed a chip onto the table. It landed squarely on number 5. The croupier spun the wheel and the few players around the table waited for his call. 'Five, red,' he shouted. Tremayne had lost 500 baht on 7, but had won 20,000 baht on his other bets. Ruby had won 18,000 baht, but she didn't seem particularly concerned.

'Randy, I'm sorry, but I'm losing interest in this game. So, if you don't mind, I think I'll try my luck at Pontoon, Blackjack, or whatever it is.'

'No, please don't go, you're bringing me luck, you must stay,' Tremayne said almost pleadingly. 'Order some more drinks, please, Ruby. Make mine a large Remy Martin.'

Tremayne returned his attention to roulette. No more 37 to 1 shots, he thought; now that he had some real money to play with he'd try the short odds. He placed 10,000 baht on the second 12 numbers—13 to 24, and 10,000 baht on Red. He watched, almost mesmerised by the spinning wheel.

'Red, 21,' the croupier almost shrieked, as he noticed Tremayne's two piles of chips. He added the winning chips and pushed them across to Tremayne, who stacked them neatly in piles.

'You're doing pretty well,' said Ruby, as she handed him a half glass of Remy Martin.

Tremayne took a swig from the glass and put his arm around Ruby's shoulders. 'Yes, my dear, and it is all due to your presence.'

The croupier called for all bets to be placed. Everyone around the table looked at Tremayne, waiting for him to make his bets.

The croupier looked worried. If this punter's luck held and they followed suit the house could be in trouble, he thought, as he pressed his emergency call button under the table.

The beaming Charlie Chan-like Cheung appeared at the croupier's side within seconds. The croupier motioned with his head towards Tremayne and Cheung's expression became inscrutable as he watched Tremayne counting chips and sipping cognac.

Tremayne looked across at Cheung and beckoned him over to his side of the table. "Charlie Chan", as he had become in Tremayne's mind, his face changing from inscrutability to one wreathed in smiles, joined Tremayne.

'Is there a problem, Mr Chan?' Tremayne asked with an edge to his voice.

'No, everything is hunky-dory, except that you are calling me "Chan" whereas my name is "Cheung",' the beaming Chinaman answered.

'That's good, I'm glad to hear that, Mr Cheung,' said Tremayne, 'You had me worried for a bit. But before I resume play, I have a question for you: what is the house's betting limit?'

Cheung looked thoughtful, licked his lips, examined his well-manicured hands, moved his weight from one foot to the other, and then with his face wreathed in smiles quietly replied, 'In your case, sir, we have no limit. The house will honour any bet you care to make.'

Tremayne turned to the table and all eyes followed his every move. He called the croupier to take in his 500 baht chips and replace them with 1,000 and 5,000 baht chips. The croupier looked at Cheung, who nodded approval.

Tremayne made ready to place his next bet. The other players and most of the customers not engaged at other tables, gathered around the table to watch intently. Tremayne placed five 5,000 baht chips each on the Black and Even squares. There was a scramble to follow his lead by the other players. The croupier had a pained look as he spun the wheel and sped the ball in the opposite direction. Apart from the noise of the whirring wheel and the noisy pitter-patter sound of the ball as it bounced around the wheel, the room was as silent as a Pharaoh's tomb. As the ball came to rest in its selected pocket everyone around the table craned their necks to see where the ball had landed. 'It's 20 black!' screamed a score, or more of excited voices, in three or four different tongues. The worried looking croupier confirmed the result and called for the assistance of a colleague to help him pay out all the winners.

Tremayne put his hand up to the croupier. 'You can let my bet ride,' he said, draining his glass and motioning to a nearby waiter for a refill. A few of the players followed suit, but most of them collected their winnings and settled to watch Tremayne's next play.

Ruby grasped Tremayne's forearm. 'Don't you think you've won enough for one evening?' she said with genuine tone of concern in her voice.

Tremayne turned to her with a smile. 'I've nearly done, my dear. A couple more bets and I'll call it a day.'

The croupier spun the wheel. Everyone watched the brief journey of the ball until it came to rest—in the 26 black slot. There was a loud gasp from the audience. Tremayne tried his best to look nonchalant, but his pulse was racing and he felt giddy with elation.

'Randy, please, no more, you're pushing your luck too far. One thing my father taught me about gambling is always quit when you're ahead!'

'Darling, I feel that this is the night when my ship finally comes home; or I'm dealt a Royal Flush in Hearts, or I find a crock of gold at the end of the rainbow. It's my destiny—I must go for broke!'

Ruby turned away. What more could she say, she thought. The man's a born loser and, sadly, he seems to be the only one who doesn't know it.

'Mr Dealer,' called Tremayne, in a parade ground voice, 'move all of those chips and the ones I have here, equally on to the Red and Odd squares.' To the waiter, now at his elbow, 'Quickly, fill my glass before he spins that wheel.'

The croupier looked, as if for guidance, towards his employer. Cheung, inscrutably faced, gently nodded. The croupier, with the trace of an enigmatic smile on his face, spun the wheel and launched the ball. The atmosphere in the room became as heavy as 1950's London smog. No one murmured. The only sound: the tantalising whirring of the wheel and the pitter-pattering of the ball. To the watchers, its 20-second journey seemed interminable. Then, hardly before the wheel had stopped and the ball about to find its home, the croupier screamed in a voice that might have cracked crystal, '22 Black!' and started to gather in the losing bets.

Tremayne stood, as if transfixed, staring at the silver ball in black pocket 22. 'Those cunning bastards have fixed the wheel, I'll be damned if I'm going to let them cheat me.'

'Randy, it's no use, you lost,' Ruby said, clutching at his arm. 'It was a bet too far! You could have gone away with a nice piece of change, but you've blown it. So let's get out of here and go back to the hotel.'

Tremayne shook her hold free and looked across at Cheung, whose inscrutable look changed to a sneer as he snapped his fingers and three of the biggest and toughest looking men in the room lined up behind him. Most of the customers, sensing trouble, melted away.

Cheung and his three henchmen moved towards Tremayne, who held his ground. 'Honourable sir, have you a complaint to make about my establishment?'

'Yes, I damn well have! Your croupier, or another of your flunkies, rigged that wheel, so everybody at the table lost.'

'I'm sorry you feel that way, sir, but I have to say that you lost fair and square. We find it unnecessary to use rigged equipment. The odds are always in favour of the house. You had a long run for your miserable amount of stake money—5,000 baht, wasn't it? Why don't you accept the fact that you are just another bad loser, who never knows when it is time to fold up his tent and go home?'

Tremayne looked hard at Cheung and his trio of bruisers. Twenty years ago, even 10 years ago, he would have taken them on, and probably wiped the floor with them, he thought—but the odds were now too great and no doubt that crafty Chinaman had got a lot more help to call on if he should need it.

'Come on, Randy, take me back to the hotel, or I shall go alone,' implored Ruby.

'Yes, honourable sir, why don't you do as the lady asks—go now, before you cause me any further displeasure, and I'm obliged to have you removed.'

Tremayne gave Cheung one last withering look that would have, in times long past, caused an officer cadet to quake in his boots. 'OK, Mr Cheung, you win this time, but you would be wise to hope that our paths never cross again,' said Tremayne, as he caught Ruby's outstretched hand and guided her to the door.

CHAPTER 13

❀

It was 5.45 a.m. and Tremayne and Ruby were sitting outside the airport departure lounge at Songkhla, waiting for Joe Swaine to complete his pre-flight airworthiness checks and refuel the Devon. Harry Simmons was in the air traffic control tower going over his flight plan with the controllers.

'Well, Ruby, have you enjoyed your brief stay in Songkhla?

'Yes, it certainly is a beautiful spot for a holiday. I would like to have stayed longer, but I have to say that you nearly spoilt it for me with all that carrying on in the casino. I'm just not used to it. I know you didn't lose very much money. Equivalent to about a £100, wasn't it, so why all the fuss? You had me quite worried, I thought you were going to take on that gang of thugs! You should have quit when you were ahead and you would have had something to show for the evening. Having said that, the evening did end rather well for both of us, didn't it? Which only goes to show that you can be relied upon to perform better on a bed than on a table.'

They both laughed loud enough for Joe to look in their direction as he finished refuelling the Devon.

Tremayne nodded. 'Of course, you are right, it was foolish of me to try to break that bank. As you say, £100 is not so very much to lose. Well, it may not be to you with your financial resources, and in normal circumstances it wouldn't be very much of a loss for me, but the fact is I owe considerably more than that to three Chinese bookies and they are all pressing me to settle my debts. If I had come away from the table before that last bet, I should have had enough left over to have taken you down to Hua Hin—the King and Queen's favourite resort—or Pattaya, a very popular resort, for a much longer break. They are not so far from Bangkok and we could have driven down in the Landrover.'

'Sounds great, and I'd love to spend some time there with you. That is, of course, provided you don't want to spend all your nights in casinos. But whatever we decide, it'll have to wait until I get back from Saigon.' Ruby suddenly looked serious. 'As to your debts, please don't be offended if I offer to lend you enough money to pay them off.'

Tremayne looked astonished. 'That's extremely generous of you to offer me financial help, but I couldn't possibly accept it.'

'Why ever not, we are lovers, aren't we? And from what you have told me your wife has shown little sympathy in the past regarding your problems, and been unwilling to make some of her considerable assets available for your use.'

I must be careful here, thought Tremayne, *I don't want to talk myself out of the loan.* 'What you say is very true, darling, but it still doesn't make it right for me, in my position, to borrow money from a young woman of such short acquaintance.'

'Short acquaintance, eh! What utter tosh! You lay me at every opportunity. You talk of getting a divorce from your wife, to marry me and yet you baulk at accepting a relatively small loan from me.'

Tremayne did his utmost to look humble. 'Well, Ruby, if you are quite sure that it would do nothing to harm our relationship, I would be everlastingly grateful for your help.'

'Of course, it won't. Now what do you need to clear the debt, in round figures, please. I'll be able to draw it from the Hong Kong and Shanghai Bank tomorrow and you can collect it from my hotel in the afternoon.'

Tremayne pretended to make some mental calculations for about ten seconds. 'One hundred and fifty-thousand baht should take care of the entire amount owing, which will include any interest they might add,' said Tremayne, mentally crossing his fingers.

'OK, I'll be at the—' said Ruby, cutting short, as Harry and Joe suddenly appeared in front of them.

'Everything is in order for takeoff in ten minutes, sir,' said Harry, gazing at Ruby with undisguised lust in his eyes.

Tremayne didn't seem to notice, but Harry's lecherous look made Ruby slightly uncomfortable and she gave him a black look as she crossed her legs and buttoned up her bush shirt to cover up the exposed deep chasm between her ample, golden-tanned breasts.

'Good, then let's get aboard, chaps,' said Tremayne in the cheeriest voice the crew had ever heard him use. 'Joe, fetch the two holdalls please and see they're stowed.'

Ruby took her seat in the passenger section, took out a large notebook from her shoulder bag and began to make notes for her article. But her mind was on other things. She fully realised that Tremayne had a problem with his weakness for gambling; some would call it an addiction. Like her father, he also drank too much, but that was probably due to his unhappy home life, and his bitterness about not having made the progress in his chosen career that he thought he should have done. She reasoned that once they were together and he was out of the service and in a less stressful job, something like managing a golf club, his desire to gamble would diminish and he would no longer need an alcoholic crutch. Despite his present weaknesses, she knew that she had fallen in love with him; she was not just infatuated with him, as she had been with so many other personable young men in her time. She could see herself married to him, provided he didn't want to change her life too much. She wasn't bothered much about their age difference. He was a man of the world, sophisticated, had an attractive persona, a commanding presence and, most importantly, he was virile and a most satisfactory bed companion.

Her thoughts were suddenly interrupted by Joe, who quietly asked: 'Would you like a cold drink, Miss Carterton? We've got Fanta, orange juice, lemonade, Singha, Heineken and San Miguel beer, and even ice cold H2O.'

Ruby treated Joe to one of her warmest smiles. 'An orange juice would be lovely.'

Joe rummaged in a large plastic bucket at the rear of the aircraft and withdrew a can dripping with water. He carefully dried and opened the can and passed it to Ruby. 'I'm sorry we don't have any glasses, just a couple of mugs. The skipper doesn't bother with them, unless we've got VIPs, or ladies on board—no offence intended to you, Miss.'

Ruby laughed softly. 'That's perfectly all right, a can is fine, Joe. You're giving me better service than I get on QANTAS.'

'Well, you should try flying with TWA more often,' Joe said with a broad grin.

'TWA? Do you mean Trans World Airlines?'

'No,' laughed Joe out loud. 'I mean Teeny Weeny Airlines—that's us!'

'Oh, I see, how quaint. I must remember to tell my father,' Ruby laughed.

'Never mind fraternizing with the passengers, Joe, what about us up front?' Tremayne called through the partially open cabin door. 'Bring me a San Miguel and a lemonade for Harry.'

'Oh, dear, I do hope I haven't got you into trouble, Joe,' said Ruby with a laugh.

'No, it's just the group captain having his little joke,' answered Joe as he rummaged through his bucket for the required drinks.

🍁 🍁 🍁

Ruby awoke suddenly to hear Tremayne calling, 'How would you like to come up front and take the controls for a bit, Ruby?'

Ruby shook her head and ran her fingers through her long silky blonde hair, more to wake herself up than to pretty herself. 'Yes, please, that would be wonderful. I've always wanted to fly an aeroplane and if I had more time I'd take flying lessons.'

Harry, a scowl on his face, came into the cabin. 'OK Miss, in you go,' he said as he sat next to Joe.

Ruby entered the flight deck and saw that Tremayne was seated in the left-hand seat, the co-pilot's—if the plane had one—or the navigator's seat. She sat in the right-hand seat and waited, as calmly as she could, for instruction. Tremayne pointed out all the major controls and dials to watch.

'The aircraft is now on autopilot. Take hold of the wheel and pull that lever on your right side, down as far as it will go. You will then have complete control of the aircraft,' ordered Tremayne in a flight instructor's voice.

The aircraft's nose went forward and the Devon dropped a thousand feet.

'Pull back the frigging stick,' ordered Tremayne with a slight tremor in his voice.

Ruby reacted sharply and, as the aircraft suddenly stopped descent and came back to level flight, she felt as though her insides were dropping out.

In the passenger section panic took hold of Harry. 'What's that crazy bastard got the girl doing? He'll get us all killed if he leaves her at the controls!'

Joe laughed, almost hysterically. 'Don't get into such a flap—it's all happened before. You should have got used to the skipper's flight instructor antics. Don't you remember when he was trying to teach his son, Peter, how to fly? He had him in such a state that the kid nearly flew us into the bloody ground!'

Harry calmed down and almost whispered, 'Sorry, Joe, you'd think that with almost 30 years flying experience, I wouldn't get in such a lather over what was not much worse than a spot of turbulence. The fact is, since flying with our group captain, I've developed a high state of nervousness when I'm flying with him. He's so unpredictable, he—'

Harry was interrupted by Tremayne's shout from the flight deck. 'Get back in here, Harry.'

Ruby, slightly flushed, came back in the passenger section and sat down.

Harry acknowledged her with a nod and went forward to join Tremayne.

'I bet you could do with something a little stronger than orange juice after that, Miss. How about a nip of this?' offered Joe, pulling a silver hip flask from his pocket. 'It's 12 year-old Scotch.'

'You, betcha, you bonzer mate,' replied Ruby, accepting the opened flask and taking a swig of the fiery spirit.

🍁   🍁   🍁

Tremayne expertly landed the Devon and taxied the aircraft to its allocated parking area, a few yards from the arrivals' lounge. He had radioed the embassy an hour before his expected arrival and was not surprised to see that Barry Marshall was sitting in the parked Landrover. But what did surprise him was to see Fiona sitting in the back of his official Humber saloon. His driver, Samarn, was pacing up and down alongside the vehicle.

Joe opened the passengers' door and helped Ruby down the steps with her holdall. Tremayne quickly intercepted Ruby as she started to walk towards his car.

'Ruby, Fiona has come to meet me, she's in the back of the car,' Tremayne whispered with a slight trace of panic in his voice. 'You'll have to go back to your hotel with Barry and the crew. If you want to go anywhere else today, or tomorrow morning, arrange it with Barry to take you. I'll come to the Nana about 2 p.m. tomorrow afternoon.'

Ruby gave a slight nod as she changed direction to walk to the Landrover, and almost whispered, 'I understand, perfectly, darling, I'll see you tomorrow afternoon.'

Barry had got out of the Landrover and was approaching the aircraft to see if any help was required from him.

Tremayne beckoned him to his side. 'Barry, I'm glad to see you got my message and telephoned Samarn to come and collect me. Did you speak to Mrs Tremayne?'

'Yes, sir, she answered the phone, and when I asked to speak to Samarn, she said he was out on an errand for her. So I asked her to tell Samarn to drive here as soon as he returned. Actually he got here before I did.'

Tremayne looked worried, momentarily. 'Barry, in addition to taking the crew back to the house, I want you to take Ruby with you and drop her off at the Nana Hotel. If she should ask you to take her anywhere else today, or tomorrow, do so without question and see that she gets back safely to her hotel, understood?'

'All right, sir, but wouldn't Miss Carterton be more comfortable in your air-conditioned car, and Samarn will have to pass the Nana Hotel.'

Tremayne's eyes flashed and his hands tightened into fists at his side. '*Flight Sergeant*, will you please do as I ask without question and get the crew and Miss Carterton back to Bangkok in double quick time.'

Barry shrugged his shoulders. 'Very well, sir, I'll be off as soon as Joe and Harry have done what they have to do with the Devon. Oh, by the way, I have left all your mail in the car with Mrs Tremayne. I hope *that's* OK, with you, sir.'

'Of course, it is,' Tremayne testily replied. 'Now get back to Bangkok as soon as you can. You don't have to worry about breaking the speed limit, the Landrover has CD plates.'

Barry nodded. 'Yes, sir, I'll put my foot down all the way.'

Barry walked quickly to the Landrover. Ruby was sitting in one of the back seats. Barry turned to her with a grin. 'We'll soon be off, Miss Carterton. I'm just waiting for the crew to get aboard.'

Ruby didn't reply but gave him a seductive smile.

Their ground-handling tasks with the Devon completed, Harry and Joe joined Barry and Ruby in the Landrover and Barry drove off at top speed.

Tremayne got into the back of the car next to Fiona. 'Hello, dear, this is a turn-up for the book, you meeting me at the airport! It's a first, isn't it?' He tried to cover his apprehension with jocularity.

Fiona gave Tremayne one of her darkest looks. 'What I have to say to you will have to wait until we get home. Unlike you, I don't wish our private affairs to be *heard, and discussed*, by your staff and our servants.' Turning to Samarn, 'Now drive us home, Samarn, as quickly as you can.'

Tremayne sighed deeply. He lit a Rothman and turned to look out of the window at the Thai peasants working in the paddy fields as the car sped along the Freedom Highway.

CHAPTER 14

❀

Tremayne looked over the top of *The Bangkok World* at Fiona seated in the far corner of their sitting room. 'Fiona, dear, when will the lunch be ready? It's 12.30 now and I have a meeting with Colonel Merkle at 2 p.m.'

Without looking up from her magazine she replied, 'It'll not be long. It's only a seafood salad. Sutep will call us when it's ready.'

She's hardly spoken a civil word to me since we left the airport yesterday, thought Tremayne. *I must try to win her round.* 'That's nice, I always enjoy your salad recipes; you're so imaginative when it comes to creating gastronomic delights.'

Fiona threw the magazine down on her side table. 'Oh, for heavens sake, don't try to soft-soap me! We've got something serious to talk about and now is as good a time as any. For starters, what was that Australian trollop doing on your aeroplane?'

Tremayne felt uneasy. What did she really know about what had been going on between himself and Ruby? 'For your information, Miss Carterton was accompanying Barney McMurchy down to the Thai-Malay border to obtain first-hand intelligence regarding Communist insurgent operations in the area. She wanted it to write an article for *The Sydney Star*, her father's newspaper.' That should satisfy her.

'Oh, I see; well, where was Barney McMurchy? He wasn't on your aeroplane when you returned? As they say, did he miss the bus?'

Bloody hell, Fiona trying to make a joke! She knew nothing really, he thought; she was just fishing, so there was no need for him to get into a sweat over this. 'Barney hadn't finished his series of lectures and wanted to stay down there for a few more days. Miss Carterton had finished her article and wanted to get back to Bangkok, because she is leaving for Saigon quite soon.'

'Not soon enough for me, I'm sick to death of hearing about her. She's the talk of our embassy as well as the Australian Embassy.'

'Look here, Fiona, I think you are making a full-blown production about nothing at all. I was just doing Barney a favour taking him down to Songkhla. I didn't have a clue about Miss Carterton until she turned up at the airport with him. Obviously, Barney wanted his border visit, and the instruction he was to give to the Thai Army to be publicised in the Australian newspapers. That sort of publicity can do an ambitious colonel's career a lot of good.'

Fiona laughed. 'My word, you service attachés certainly stick together. If I'm any judge of men, Barney McMurchy probably took that woman down to Songkhla for a bit of extramarital nooky. He's a typical Australian macho man—full of hormones and ready to jump into bed with *any* woman he takes a fancy to. I really do feel sorry for his poor wife, Nora.'

Tremayne gave a silent sigh of relief. He was off the hook—the silly bitch thought Barney and Ruby were playing away from home! There was no percentage in him defending Barney—he'd let Fiona think what she liked about him. Before Tremayne could think of a suitable reply to Fiona's vindictive indictment of Barney, Sutep entered the sitting room and announced, 'Master, Madame, runcheon is leady.'

There was little conversation between them during the hurried meal. Fiona had said that she was attending a farewell party for the US Naval Attaché's wife, and that she would like the use of the official car to take her to the party at about 3 p.m. Tremayne nodded his agreement.

🍁 🍁 🍁

'Drive me to the *Satahn toot ungrit*, Samarn,' said Tremayne as he tossed his now empty briefcase onto the back seat of his official car. 'I have some papers to pick up at the embassy before I go to a meeting at the US Embassy. You need not wait for me. I shall get an embassy driver to take me to the US Embassy. You are to go straight back to the house and be available to take madam to wherever she wants to go this afternoon.'

Samarn, a retired Thai Army corporal, gave a smart salute. 'I understand, Master, I shall do as you say.'

That was nicely arranged, thought Tremayne. It would have been foolhardy for him to get Samarn to drive him to the Nana Hotel. It could get back to Fiona. She had a habit of questioning Samarn about his movements. He could walk to the Nana Hotel—it was only a stone's throw from the embassy. Tremayne comforted himself in the knowledge that he had successfully, or so he thought, deceived Fiona for most of their married life.

Arriving at the Nana Hotel, Tremayne was pleased to note that the duty receptionist was unknown to him. 'Would you ring Miss Carterton and tell her that Colonel McMurchy is here to see her?' he lied inspiredly. He guessed that the receptionist would not know the difference between an RAF officer's uniform and that of an Australian Army officer's uniform. Anyway, it was unlikely that she had ever seen an Australian colonel wearing uniform in the hotel.

The receptionist rang Ruby's room and relayed his message. 'Miss Carterton says you can go up. She is in room 307.'

Tremayne smiled to himself, thinking that after the time he had spent with Ruby in that room he would not be likely ever to forget its number. He thanked the receptionist and took the lift to Ruby's floor. Ruby must have been waiting at the door, for as soon as he lightly tapped on it she opened it.

Tremayne quickly entered, dropped his briefcase on the floor, took her into his arms, and kissed her passionately on the lips. Ruby responded and their searching tongues met. Her firm breasts pressed against his chest and for a moment Tremayne forgot the purpose of his visit and started to move her backwards towards her sensually inviting black silken-sheeted bed.

Ruby, aware of his intention, almost flung herself back on the bed, but suddenly stood firm. 'Save that for later, lover, it's business before pleasure. *Colonel McMurchy*, indeed! You artful old fox, I know your game,' said Ruby with a laugh.

Tremayne released her and they both sat down on a sofa.

'My use of Barney's name to gain admittance was simply a subterfuge to cover my tracks, my dear. Fiona seems to be fast coming to the conclusion that you and McMurchy are having some sort of affair. So I thought I should take advantage of the situation.'

Ruby gave a little frown. 'Well, I can't say that I am particularly flattered that anyone should think that I've fallen for that horny old goat, but I suppose it will divert Fiona's attention from us. Now let's get this money thing sorted.'

'Oh, so, you've been to the bank and drawn money out for me? I was very worried when I thought of you carrying all that money from the bank. Did Barry Marshall bring you back to the hotel?'

'Yes, he did, and he behaved like a perfect gentleman and so discreet. You're lucky to have such a man as your personal assistant. I hope you treat him well.'

'Yes, Barry's OK, I suppose. But he can be a bit of an old woman at times, always worrying about doing the *right* and honourable thing. I can imagine him being a bit of disciplinarian with his subordinates, too. He comes across as being somewhere between Sister Teresa and Captain Bligh. But that's enough about my staff. What I need to know is, are you quite sure you want to make this loan to me.'

'Rhubarb, Randy, of course I'm sure. I want to get you out of the clutches of your creditors. I know how ruthless these people can be to gamblers who default on paying up for their losses. So say no more about it.'

'I can't thank you enough, Ruby. You're a lifesaver. I'll see you get it back as soon as I can.'

'Good, but don't worry about it anymore. Anyway, I see you've brought a brief case. It should be big enough to accommodate that little lot.' Ruby pointed to a bulky brown paper bag on an occasional table against the wall. 'One hundred and fifty thousand baht makes quite a bundle. Better get it stowed in the brief case before we do anything else.'

'What else had you in mind, Miss Carterton?' said Tremayne with undisguised lechery.

Ruby looked serious. 'There are two things I have to tell you. This place was crawling with RAF men last night. I believe they're up from Singapore and stopping for a couple of days, before they fly off. I heard a couple of them talking about you in the bar last night and they weren't being very complimentary. One mentioned that he knew you when you were the Wing Commander Flying at RAF Brize Norton. He said that you were a "pig's orphan" to work under. The other said he knew you were here as the air attaché. Now, if these men, or any others like them, were to see us together in this hotel, any resultant gossip could find its way to Fiona. And you wouldn't want that to happen, would you?'

'No, I bloody well wouldn't. To avoid the possibility of that happening, the only answer is for you to move to another hotel, away from the embassy.'

Ruby tossed her long blonde hair back. 'Yes, but where? You know all the hotels in Bangkok, so what would you suggest?'

Tremayne looked thoughtful for a moment. 'Have you heard of the Oriental Hotel? It's a delightfully romantic hotel, which overlooks the Chao Phraya River. You, being a journalist, should feel right at home there. Many famous writers have stayed there. It's also very expensive, so it's not the sort of place that servicemen would choose to stay.'

'Yes, I've heard of that hotel. My father stayed there once. He said it was the Bangkok hotel most favoured by Somerset Maugham. A good choice; I'll telephone for a booking later and move there first thing in the morning.'

'Now that is settled, what was the other matter you wanted to talk about?'

Ruby looked unhappy. 'I received an encrypted cable from my father this morning. It came via the Australian Embassy. My father says he wants me to get over to Saigon within the next few days. Apparently our troops are moving north to link up with forward US units. He thinks they are preparing to mount a strong attack. He says it's all hush hush, and I shouldn't talk to anyone about it. You won't mention this to anyone, will you, Randy?'

'Of course not, darling, secrets *are* my business. It might be my job to steal the military secrets of my country's potential enemies, but I am cleared to the highest level to safeguard not only our own secrets, but also those of our friends and allies.'

'I'm pleased to hear that. Now why don't you get that money put in your briefcase and join me in an afternoon nap before you have to return to that dreary old embassy. Put the briefcase under the bed. It'll be quite safe there while we are lying on the bed.' Ruby slipped off her blouse, undid her belt and let her slacks slip around her ankles. Her flesh coloured bra and briefs soon joined her slacks on the floor.

Tremayne hastily stuffed the bundles of Thai currency into his briefcase and pushed it under the bed with his foot. He quickly stripped off his uniform and dropped on the bed alongside Ruby. *For all I care, Fiona can fuck herself. This is the woman for me,* he thought, as his eager hands started to explore every curve and fissure of Ruby's voluptuous body. Ruby moaned softly, 'I'm ready for you now, darling. Make it last as long as you can.'

CHAPTER 15

❦

'Thank you, Samarn, please pick me up at about five o'clock,' said Mrs Fiona Tremayne as she stepped out of the official car.

Mrs Ruth Merkle, the party hostess and Judith Cranston, the wife of the US Naval Attaché, were standing on the terrace welcoming guests. The 'afternoon soiree', as Mrs Merkle had described it, was a gathering of the US Embassy staff wives to say farewell to the naval attaché's wife. She and her husband were returning to the USA after his tour of duty in Bangkok.

Fiona was the only British person to be invited. Her invite was a matter of protocol, she being the wife of the longest serving attaché—the Doyen of the Military Attaché Corps.

Ruth Merkle, the glamorous and witty wife of the US Defence and Air Attaché, stepped forward to greet Fiona. 'Welcome aboard, Fiona, it's so nice to see you. There's no need for me to introduce Judith, or for that matter, anyone else that'll be attending this party. You've been in Bangkok so long that you must know just about everybody who's anybody.'

Fiona gave her a smile. The 'welcome aboard', thought Fiona, was probably for the benefit of Judith Cranston, a navy wife, through and through. 'Yes, almost four years, and I shan't be sorry to leave.'

Judith Cranston raised her eyebrows. 'After four years, I can well understand you wanting to get back to your home in

England, Fiona. We've only been here two years and that seems forever. I'm homesick for Virginia. But I guess we're lucky my husband has been appointed to a very senior position at the Naval Academy at Annapolis, Maryland, which is quite near our home in Richmond, Virginia, and very near Washington D.C.'

'How very nice for you both,' said Fiona, thinking some people have all the luck. Judith's not yet forty, her husband's not much older and he's well on his way to becoming an admiral.

All the guests present and provided with cocktails, the wives settled in groups at different tables. Fiona found herself seated with Ruth Merkle, Judith Cranston and Doris Dacres, the military attaché's wife.

'It's rather a coincidence, us being together today, Ruth, when our husbands are attending a meeting together at your embassy,' said Fiona for something to say in the context of what was, for her, fast becoming a boring conversation.

Ruth laughed. 'The only meeting Harold is attending today is a golf tournament. He's playing with the JUSMAG team against the Royal Thai Army team.'

'Oh, really!' Fiona exclaimed, nearly swallowing the olive in her martini. 'I could have sworn that Randy said he was meeting with Harold at your embassy this afternoon. I must have misheard him. He goes to so many meetings. It was probably something at SEATO.'

'From what I hear, Fiona, your husband is always attending some meeting or other,' said Judith Cranston, meaningfully. 'There seems to be a great demand for his services. I suppose it's because of his position as the Doyen of the Attaché Corps.'

Bitch! Thought Fiona. *What is she trying to suggest? But if those golf clubs of his are in the boot of our car he's got some explaining to do.*

Ruth called her housemaid to the table. The tiny, elfin-faced maid, with a silver tray of ready mixed drinks, stood, with her head bowed in respect, next to Ruth. Had she been working for a Thai employer she would have knelt down on the floor, but because of her diminutive size, she was not as tall as any of the guests who were sitting down.

'What'll you have, girls?' Ruth asked.

'Same again, please,' said Judith and Doris in chorus.

'Nothing more for me, thank you. I must be getting back to my house. I'm expecting a phone call from Switzerland from my daughter,' Fiona lied as she rose to leave.

'Oh, dear, I am sorry you have to leave so early,' replied Ruth as she rose to say goodbye to Fiona. 'Although Harold and I have no children, I do understand how necessary it is to keep in touch with your children when you are living apart.'

'Goodbye, Judith,' said Fiona with a wicked smile. 'I hope you will have an enjoyable time with all those young cadet naval officers at Annapolis. Goodbye, Doris, no doubt we'll be meeting again quite soon, and thank you Ruth for a very pleasant afternoon. It's been a most enlightening experience.'

'Goodbye, Fiona,' called Judith and Doris in chorus as Fiona walked towards her waiting car.

Samarn jumped out of his seat and opened the rear door for Fiona, who got in and sat down. 'Samarn, before we leave, would you please open the car boot and see if the master's golf clubs are in there?'

Samarn went around to the rear of the vehicle and opened the boot. 'Yes, madam, they are there, where the master always leaves them.'

'Thank you, Samarn, now please drive me back to the house,' said Fiona, her face a picture of malevolence.

CHAPTER 16

Tremayne awoke with a start and looked at his Rolex. Hell! 17.35—he'd been asleep for a couple of hours, he thought, as he turned to see Ruby asleep at his side. Her long blonde hair was in a tumble over her finely formed features.

He got out of bed and walked to the bathroom. Ruby heard him moving and awoke. 'Wait for me darling; I'll join you in the shower. Think of the water we'll save. My, my, you are a big boy when you stand naked like that,' she said, jumping out of bed, running across the room and throwing her arms around his neck.

Tremayne seized her under her buttocks and lifted her bodily into the shower stall. He turned on the water and held her in his arms as the warm water cascaded over their bodies. They stayed for several minutes soaping each other's most private parts.

'Darling, as much as I enjoy playing with you like this, I must get home before Fiona takes it into her head to ring Ruth Merkle, to see if her husband is back from his meeting.'

Ruby pretended to sulk and released her hold on his hardening member. 'Very well, if you must leave when things seem to be on the up and up again, you must. Don't forget, from tomorrow I shall be staying at the Oriental Hotel. Room 307 was vacant, so I booked it.' She gave him a come-hither look.

Tremayne kissed her still wet lips, grabbed a towel from the rail, dried himself and quickly dressed. He retrieved his briefcase from under the bed, opened it and checked its contents.

'It's all there, isn't it?' said Ruby as she emerged from the bathroom and stood naked with a towel in her hand.

Tremayne shut the briefcase with a sheepish look on his face. 'Yes, of course, but you can't be too careful. You never know who might have entered this room while we were asleep.'

'Oh, I suppose so, but in my experience I have found Thais to be honourable and honest people.'

'Yes, most of them are, but in my business you quickly learn *not* to trust anyone too much,' said Tremayne as he moved to the door.

Ruby, now dressed in her flesh coloured bra and miniscule briefs, followed him to the door.

Tremayne clasped her to him with his disengaged arm and kissed her fiercely on the mouth. 'Now I *must* go,' he said opening the door and walking out into the corridor.

'Goodbye, darling, and don't forget—pay off those bookies as soon as you can.'

Tremayne gave Ruby a "thumbs up" sign as he strode purposefully down the corridor.

❦   ❦   ❦

So she's back, thought Tremayne, as he noticed Samarn cleaning the official car in front of the four-car garage at the side of the house. He let himself in and quietly crept upstairs and went to the master bedroom. He must hide this money somewhere and replace the normal contents of his briefcase. He emptied the banknotes onto the bed and went to his wardrobe to retrieve the items he normally carried in the briefcase. The flushing of the lavatory cistern in the en suite bathroom caused him to drop the briefcase in alarm. What to do? Get the money back into the briefcase before Fiona came out of the bathroom. It couldn't be anyone else, the servants were forbidden to use the inside toilets. He grabbed the briefcase off the floor and scrambled over to the bed—too late!

Fiona, calm and unshaken, walked across the room and looked down at the pile of money on the bed. 'Where did you get all this money? Have you robbed a bank, Randolph?' she asked, without a trace of humour on her face.

Tremayne forced a laugh. 'Of course not, dear, I've a confession to make to you. I didn't go to a meeting at the US Embassy and I've been playing in a golf tournament this afternoon. All the players in the tournament put 5,000 baht into a pool as prize money, for the first, second and third place winners. And, you'd never guess, but I won first prize—150,000 baht!'

'Well, that was a wonderful piece of luck for you, especially when you play off a handicap of 16, whereas most of the US Embassy diplomats, JUSMAG officers and Thai military players have single figure handicaps!'

'That may be so, Fiona, but if you'd have seen my performance you would have been proud of your husband. I went round in 75, with two birdies and a hole in one!'

'Randolph, dear, you might think you can play golf as well as Ben Hogan, but I know better. Since you started playing you've never been round a golf course in less than 84 strokes!'

Tremayne avoided Fiona's gaze by opening his wardrobe to look for a shoebox to put the money in.

Fiona watched him placing the money neatly in a shoebox. 'But speaking of handicaps, you were surely very much handicapped playing without golf clubs. What did you use—broom handles!'

'Damnation!' Tremayne silently cursed, 'the bitch knows something; she must have seen the blasted clubs in the boot. What now? She knows I'd never play in a tournament with borrowed clubs. My only hope is another confession, nearer to the truth.' Tremayne sat down on the bed, folded his arms and looked at Fiona with the best apologetic expression he could muster. 'I'm really sorry for all the lies I've been telling you about this money. The simple truth is, I won it gambling at roulette over the last few weeks. But knowing how much you are against me gambling, I thought it better not to tell you. It was my intention to use some of this money to buy you a ticket for a flight to London, to visit Peter at his school in Rutland.'

What sort of fool does this man take me for? He could never have accumulated all this money from gambling. He'd have gambled with it until he had lost the lot, as he has always done. I'll string him along for a bit and teach him a lesson he'll not forget in a hurry, Fiona conspired in her mind.

'Oh, Randolph, what a lovely surprise, and there was me thinking all sorts of preposterous things about you and your gambling and almost believing that you were having some sort of affair with that Australian tart. It seems I owe you an apology.'

Tremayne forced a smile, took her by the hand and pulled her down next to him on the bed. 'Forget it, darling; you had every right to doubt me. It is I who should be apologising to you for my cavalier behaviour these last few weeks.'

Fiona squeezed his hand and looked up into his eyes. 'Well, my dear, why not let us make it a family affair. You've got the equivalent of about 3,000 pounds here, enough money to take us all to London. You could send some to Daphne to fly there to meet us. We could then go up to Rutland to collect Peter and take him back to London to have a real holiday. We could stay at the Dorchester, you know how much you like that hotel; we could see some West

End shows; visit relatives and friends, and live it up for about a month. After all, you know what they say—easy come, easy go!'

Tremayne suddenly felt as though he was going to be sick. His stomach churned over and, in spite of the coolness of the air-conditioned room, he could feel his body exuding perspiration. He released his hand from her hold and got off the bed. 'Excuse me, Fiona, I must get a glass of water. I think I've got a touch of that dengue fever returning.'

'Oh, you poor dear,' said Fiona, in sympathetic voice. 'I'll get you those tablets that Doctor Herschmeir prescribed for the fever.'

Fiona left the room to look for the tablets downstairs. Tremayne could hear her calling out to the maids: 'Have any of you seen the master's dengue tablets, he's...'

Tremayne stumbled into the bathroom and closed the door. Looking into the mirror he saw a haggard face, with bloodshot eyes and beads of perspiration running down his forehead. *She's got me over a barrel, the crafty cow! How do I get out of this one? What she wants us to do would take up most of the money. If I let her have her way, I'll not have enough to pay off my gambling debts. Of course I can't go with her. I want these next few days with Ruby, before she goes to Saigon. Aha, that's one good thing that could come out of all this. I'll stay here and let Fiona go to London. I'll then be able to see Ruby as often and as long as I like without raising any suspicion in Fiona's mind.* He heard Fiona returning and joined her in the bedroom.

'Here, Randolph, take two of these with water,' Fiona said, handing him the tablets and a glass of water.

Tremayne did as he was instructed and made an effort to regain his normal composure. 'Thank you, dear, I'm beginning to feel much better now.'

'That's good; you have a lie down and rest before dinner, and I'll get on to BOAC to see what flights they have available during the next day or two. We shouldn't have too much trouble; there are usually plenty of first class seats available on most flights.'

It gets worse, thought, Tremayne. 'Just, a minute, Fiona, before you start booking seats, you'll have to count me out. It would be impossible for me to leave at such short notice. And I didn't mention it before, but the newly appointed Commander-in-Chief, Far East Air Force is paying a courtesy visit to Bangkok and will expect me to accompany him when he calls on the SEATO country ambassadors and local representatives, and Thai military commanders. No, I'm afraid there's no chance at all of me being able to be away from Bangkok during the next few weeks. But, there's no reason why we can't revert to Plan A, and for you to do all you want to do with the children, but without me.'

Fiona looked thoughtful. 'Well, that being the case, I'll go ahead and make the necessary arrangements,' she said as she picked up the shoebox of money.

Tremayne's stomach churned again. 'What are you going to do with that money?' he croaked.

'Bank it, of course,' said Fiona testily. 'We can't have all this money in the house. I'll get Samarn to take me to the Hong Kong and Shanghai Bank first thing in the morning. Anyway, I shall need it in the bank, to draw on it to pay for the flights, and send money to Daphne and Peter.'

Fiona left him in the bedroom. *That's me then, up crap creek without a paddle*, thought Tremayne, as he reached into the bottom of his wardrobe for a bottle of Remy Martin.

CHAPTER 17

Tremayne walked into his office, sat at his desk, opened his briefcase, took out a packet of Rothmans and lit a cigarette. *Well, that's her out of the way for about a month,* he thought as he drew deeply on his cigarette. *Now I can get to see Ruby without having to concoct alibis for Fiona. She's not left much of Ruby's loan in the joint bank account, but no matter, my creditors haven't been bothering me lately.*

'Barry!' shouted Tremayne, without opening his door. 'You can fetch the mail in now.'

Barry entered with an armful of papers and files. 'Good morning, sir, did Mrs Tremayne get away all right?'

'Morning, Barry, yes she's well on her way to Singapore by now. What have we got this morning, anything I need to see? I want to keep my desk clear for the next few days. I've got rather a lot of people to see before the new Commander-in-Chief, FEAF, pays his visit, so don't bother me with anything that you can deal with.

Barry held on to the morning's mail. 'Well, you'll not need to see any of this then, sir. There is just one thing, though—the 5,000 baht, you owe the imprest account. Can you let me have it now?'

Tremayne looked slightly peeved, but rummaged through his briefcase and laid his cheque book on his desk and reached for his fountain pen.

Barry looked surprised. 'It would be better, sir, if you paid cash. A personal cheque from you paid into the imprest bank account might result in an adverse observation by the MoD auditors.'

'Oh, fuck the bloody MoD auditors,' snarled Tremayne, 'I'll make the cheque out to you and you can cash it and put the money in your cash box.'

Barry frowned. 'Very well, sir, if that's what you want, I'll take your cheque.'

Tremayne scribbled out the cheque and tossed it across his desk. Barry picked it up and remained standing in front of Tremayne's desk.

'Anything else?' snapped Tremayne testily.

'Yes, sir, there is. You had a caller whilst you were seeing Mrs Tremayne off. The man, Chinese, I think, was an ugly looking customer. Not like any of your usual callers. He said he was very anxious to see you on a very personal matter. I told him you weren't available and asked for his business card so that I could telephone him when you were available to see him. He didn't have one, but said his name was Ho Ming. I explained to him that embassy staff did not normally conduct their personal affairs at the embassy and that he would be better advised to call at your home, late afternoon or early evening. A time that I thought you would be available to see him.'

Tremayne didn't recognise the name, but from what Barry had said, he could only guess that the man was some sort of debt collector for one of the gambling houses he frequented. *I must play this one very cool.* 'OK, Barry, thank you, I'll see whoever he is when he calls at my home. He's probably just one of those finance business touts trying to get me to invest with them. Bangkok's crawling with them; we've even had them badgering members at the British Club.'

Barry grinned. 'Yes, I know, we had one, a Dutchman, call at the staff house a few days ago. He promised us ridiculous returns on any investments we made. Joe told him to piss off!'

Tremayne laughed. 'Yes, I can imagine Joe telling him that. Now you can get on with what you've got to do. I shan't be in after luncheon. I got an appointment with the RTAF Senior Air Staff Officer, to discuss the future use of Leong Nok Tha.'

'That's not in my diary, sir. Have you got the right date?'

'Yes, I only arranged it yesterday and didn't bother to tell you.'

Barry gave a silent tut and returned to the general office. Tremayne rang the Oriental Hotel and asked the switchboard operator to connect him with Room 307.

CHAPTER 18

❁

'Master, a Chinese gentleman come see you. He say he Mr Ho Ming. I tell him wait at door. Shall I ask him in?'

Tremayne lowered his *Bangkok Post* to the floor and placed his glass of Remy Martin on his side table. 'No, Nong, I'll see him at the door.'

Tremayne waited until Nong had returned to the servants' kitchen and went to the front entrance. The man was, as Barry had described him, a very ugly customer. He was dressed entirely in black, and carried a black cane. He was no more than average height, but his shoulders were almost as wide as the front door. He smiled, which did nothing to improve his ugly features.

Tremayne approached him, ignoring his outstretched hand. 'Yes, what can I do for you?'

The man smiled again. 'My name is Ho Ming and I work for Mr Han Woo. He has sent me to collect the money you owe him—138,000 baht!'

Tremayne gasped. 'Nonsense, I don't owe anyone that amount of money.'

'That was the case, sir, before Mr Woo bought your IOUs from two other casino owners, and added the amount you owed them, to that which you owe him,' Ho Ming explained, as if he were addressing a child.

'Oh, I see. So now I owe Mr Woo 138,000 baht.'

'Yes, sir,' said Ming, still smiling, 'that is so. But he instructed me to tell you that this amount will increase by ten per cent for every day that the debt is outstanding.'

Tremayne looked worried and turned and looked down the passage to the servants' kitchen. 'I think we had better go into my study to discuss this matter. I don't want to risk my servants eavesdropping on our conversation.'

Ho Ming shrugged his massive shoulders. 'Just as you wish, sir, but as I see it there is little to discuss. You owe Mr Woo 138,000 baht and he wants it now. I would urge you to make this payment or incur the extreme displeasure of Mr Woo, which might result in an unpleasant occurrence befalling you.'

Tremayne led the way to his study and closed the door behind them. 'Take a seat Mr Ming,' said Tremayne, pointing to a leather chesterfield chair next to his desk. Ming sat down and leant his cane against the side of the desk. 'Can I offer you a cognac, Mr Ming? It's Remy Martin, a favourite of mine. I'm sure you'd like it.'

'Yes, please, I would. I've heard of it, and have often been tempted to try it, but it is far too expensive for ordinary working people to buy in Thailand. I suppose you can buy it at duty free prices from your embassy commissary.'

'That's right, it's one of the few perks of the job,' said Tremayne, as he opened his desk drawer and lifted a bottle of Remy Martin and two balloon glasses out of the drawer and placed them on the desk. He opened the bottle and poured a quadruple measure into each glass.

Ming watched his every movement, thinking that perhaps he wouldn't have as much trouble collecting from this man as he had been led to believe.

Tremayne passed one of the glasses across the desk. Ming smacked his lips as he leant forward to pick it up. Tremayne picked up the near empty bottle and hit Ming on his left temple.

The blow burst a vein in Ming's temple and blood spurted across the desk, staining the desk blotter. Ming shook his head and as he fell back into the chesterfield chair, his right hand shot under his left armpit. *He's carrying a pistol*, Tremayne realised, as he grabbed up a paper knife from his desk, leant over and plunged the knife into Ming's right eye. Ming gave a short, sharp scream, as the long, thin, Thai bronze blade tore through his eye and entered his brain, and he flopped across the arm of the chair.

Tremayne went around the desk and felt for a pulse in Ming's limp wrist. There was none. The man was dead.

Now to clear up, thought Tremayne. He mopped up the blood that had fallen on the highly polished wooden floor with sheets of blotting paper. Thankfully no stained carpets to explain away.

He collected a thick bath towel from the downstairs loo and wrapped it around Ming's head. He removed the dead man's jacket and found that he was wearing a shoulder holster containing a Japanese Nambu, 7.65 mm, automatic pistol and a spare eight round magazine. There was a stiletto strapped in a sheath to his left arm. His black cane, as Tremayne had suspected, was a swordstick.

He went through the man's pockets. Some loose change, a cigarette lighter, a crumbled packet of Thai cigarettes and a small bunch of keys. The leather wallet in his hip pocket contained about one thousand baht in small notes, a finger-stained photograph of a nude Thai girl in an erotic pose, and a membership card for the Lucky Strike casino. He transferred the money to his own wallet; tore up the pornographic photograph and membership card and burnt them in an ashtray. He put Ming's keys in his desk drawer.

Although he didn't think any of the servants had heard the noise above the sound of the television they would be watching in the servants' kitchen at the rear of the house, he locked the study door before he went out through the French doors and walked to the garage. There was a large waterproof sheet for covering the garden furniture during the rainy season, stored in the garage. He took the sheet back into the study and laid the body on it. He put the wallet, cigarette lighter and cigarettes in the man's jacket pockets. Stripping off the rest of the man's clothing, he bundled it all together. *Something I can jettison from the aircraft, when I'm next flying*, he thought. He wrapped the sheet tightly around the body and tied it together with string from a ball he had in his desk. *Now, where to hide the body? Ah, I know, in the deep klong that runs alongside the garden at the other side of the garage.*

Tremayne dragged the body across the room and into the garden and over to the side of the bank of the klong. What he needed was something to weigh it down. A small stone Buddha stature that stood in the middle of the garden would serve the purpose., he thought. He tied the stature to the human bundle and gently pushed it into the dark, muddy and weed-filled waters of the klong.

He placed the bundle of Ming's clothing in a sack he found in the gardener's shed and put the sack in the boot of his official car.

After that I deserve a drink and then a shower, he thought, as he walked back through the study French doors. *But before I do, I'd better check if he came in his own car and parked it near the house.* Tremayne went out on the road. There was no car parked in sight of the house. Ming must have arrived by taxi.

There was still Ming's personal armoury to dispose of. *No, I'll not get rid of them. I've a notion I might need them*, thought Tremayne as he drank both glasses of cognac that stood untouched on his desk.

CHAPTER 19

❀

'Barry, come in here a minute!' shouted Tremayne from his office.

Barry sighed deeply. *What does the miserable sod want now? He's been like a bear with a sore head for a couple of days.* Arming himself with his shorthand notebook and two HB pencils, Barry entered Tremayne's office and stood in front of his desk. 'Good morning, sir.' Whatever one thought of one's boss, the observance of the social niceties was mandatory for survival in the Diplomatic Service.

Tremayne looked up at Barry, and stubbed out his cigarette as though he were trying to make a hole in the ashtray. 'Morning, Barry,' he grunted. 'I suppose you are aware that the newly appointed Commander-in-Chief, FEAF is making a courtesy visit to Bangkok on Monday?'

'Yes, sir, I did read the HQ MEAF signal about his arrival. I understand he'll be here for three days. I've already booked a suite of rooms for him and his personal staff officer and aide-de-camp at the Erawan Hotel. I thought that it would be the most suitable hotel for the C-in-C. It is the nearest five-star rated hotel to the embassy.'

Tremayne looked surprised. 'Splendid, a good choice—that's a start. But, more importantly, there is a visit programme to be prepared. You won't have done that, will you?'

'No, sir, I presumed that you would want to provide the details of his calls and other necessary information and let me have them to produce a suitable programme.'

Tremayne frowned. 'Of course, I'm forgetting, you weren't here the last time we had a change of command. That must be more than two years ago. At that time I prepared a comprehensive programme, which pleased all concerned. It will do admirably for this visit. Pull it from the "VIP Visits" file and let me have it, so that I can check if it will need amendment.'

'Are you saying that this non-policy document—a visit programme—is over two years old, sir?'

Tremayne looked annoyed. 'Yes, of course it is, but what's that got to do with anything?'

'Only that it would have been destroyed, along with all other non-policy papers that are over two years old and no longer in current use.'

'Destroyed? How? Where? Why?' Tremayne roared.

'It will have been burnt in the embassy incinerator, in accordance with Ministry of Defence, Directorate of Intelligence instructions, contained in the standing orders for military attaché staffs.

Tremayne's eyes nearly popped from his head. 'You bloody numbskull! Do you realise what you've done? You've made it necessary for me to have to redraft a completely new programme. What have you got to say for yourself?'

Barry straightened himself up to his full height and looked down at Tremayne. 'Sir, when I was receiving my security briefings at the MoD in preparation for taking up this post, great emphasis was placed on the need for the secure custody, use and transmission of all files and documents regardless of their security grading. It was explained to me that files and documents, which had been superseded, or considered to be of no further interest, should be destroyed by fire and their ashes broken up. The reason for this was that should the embassy come under attack by local insurgents, or invading forces, there might not be time for the disposal of such documents before the embassy was sacked and staff were evacuated, which might result in documents falling into the hands of enemies or potential enemies of Britain.'

Tremayne sat still in his chair, looking with a fixed gaze at Barry, as if mesmerised by Barry's outpouring, of what he would call "administrative bullshit".

Barry paused for breathe and then continued relentlessly. 'You will not be aware, but when I first came here I found that our filing cabinets in the strong room were full of yellowing files and documents, which had long passed the time when they should have been destroyed. I spent several of my Saturday mornings coming to the embassy when it was closed to sort out the filing system and burn all the files no longer required. However, despite the mammoth task I found I had taken on, I ensured that the titles and full details of the contents of these files were properly recorded on the appropriate forms in accordance with the Public Records Act, 1960. Would you care to see the records of all those files and documents that have been destroyed?'

Tremayne's faced purpled. 'No, I certainly would not, and if you utter another word about the Public Records Act, or the security of files, I'll have you shipped back to the UK for gross insubordination! Now sit in that chair and take dictation!'

🍁   🍁   🍁

Barry was returning from the duplicating room, with copies of the new programme for distribution. Roy Hughes stopped him in the corridor. 'What was all that commotion in Tremayne's office about? Was the group captain giving you another telling off? He certainly seemed to be having a good go at you.'

Barry didn't see why he should confide in Hughes, but he didn't want him to get the idea that he was always in trouble with Tremayne. He explained briefly what had caused Tremayne's outburst.

Hughes looked thoughtful. 'Well, you are certainly right about the requirements of the Public Records Act, 1960. I can well remember the briefing I received at MoD (Navy). I was told much the same as you, and a great deal more. The way the intelligence officers went on about embassy security, our responsibilities to the job, and the need for us to be careful about developing questionable relationships with the local inhabitants, made me think that the briefing was rather over-the-top. It's not as though Thailand is behind the Iron Curtain, or even the Bamboo Curtain.'

Barry grinned wickedly. 'Yes, I'm sure that MoD (Navy), the Foreign Office and MI5, would have shown great concern about security in naval attachés' offices, especially after one of your MoD (Navy) civil servants had got himself *compromised* by the KGB in Moscow.'

Hughes' face reddened. 'I suppose you are referring to John Vassall, the naval attaché's assistant in Moscow in the 1950's?'

'I certainly am. He's the bloody homo who was the cause of the wastepaper basket searching by embassy guards and the need to remove your typewriter ribbon when you left the office unattended. I hadn't been here more than a few weeks when I was up in front of the Head of Chancery for putting a torn-up signal in my wastepaper bin. It was only classified "restricted". Its subject: "Instructions for RAF personnel wishing to go on leave to Rhodesia, in the wake of the Rhodesian Government declaring unilateral independence." That's what I call over-the-top.'

Hughes nodded sagely. 'Yes, I suppose it is, but there is a real need for tight security in embassies, for however tight the country's security is, there'll always be people who'll try to get away with selling our nation's secrets because they have been compromised in "honey-traps", or tempted by the rewards offered by foreign secret service agencies for treasonable acts in disclosing our nation's secrets.'

'Too right,' said Barry, 'but I must get back to the office, before my irascible master arranges to have me court-martialled for burning his damned visit file.'

CHAPTER 20

Tremayne walked to where Samarn usually parked the official car in the embassy compound. It was there. Tremayne could see Samarn sitting bolt upright in the driver's seat. Odd, he thought, for when Samarn was on his own in the car waiting for his passengers he would be relaxed, even dozing; but would spring to life as soon as anyone approached the car, and leap out of the car to open the rear door if it were Tremayne, or any member of his family, who approached. But Samarn had not turned around, or even moved. Tremayne put his hand on the handle of the rear door. As he did so the door swung open and he saw two men sitting in the back of the car. The one nearest the open door, a young Thai, or Laotian, held an automatic pistol, fitted with a sound moderator, which was pointed unwaveringly at Tremayne's midriff.

'Please get in the front seat next to your driver, Group Captain Tremayne,' ordered the voice of the other man, who was partially shielded by the gunman. It was Han Woo, the owner of the Lucky Strike Casino.

Tremayne thought of calling the Gurkha guard from the main gate, but he would be unarmed, and the gun held on him was a good enough reason to do as he was ordered and see what opportunity to escape, or overcome his adversaries, might occur later. He opened the front door and sat down next to the still unmoving Samarn.

'That's right, group captain, this is no time for heroics. You do exactly as I ask and you will stay alive,' said Woo without a trace of menace in his tone. 'Now pass your briefcase over the back of the seat.'

Tremayne passed it over and Woo placed it on the floor between his legs.

'Now, group captain, tell your driver to drive to my casino. He knows the way, he's driven you there often enough.'

Samarn turned to face Tremayne, a questioning look on his face. Tremayne shook his head, and turned around to face Woo. 'You can't expect to get away with this—threatening an accredited diplomat!'

'Be quiet, group captain, and do as I say. Tell your driver to go—now!'

The gunman prodded Tremayne in the back with his pistol for emphasis.

Tremayne turned to Samarn, and nodded. Samarn released the handbrake and drove the car slowly towards the gate. Woo and his henchman ducked their heads down behind the seat as Samarn slowly drove the car through the gate. The Gurkha guard saluted as he recognised the air attaché's car. Tremayne returned the salute without taking his eyes off the road ahead. Clear of the gate and Woo and the young gunman sat up.

Without turning to face Woo, Tremayne said, 'What is this all about? If it's about the 138,000 baht I owed you, I gave it to your Mr Ming—three days ago.'

'Please be quiet, you will find out what it is all about when we reach my casino.'

Less than 15 minutes later Samarn stopped the car at the front of the casino.

Woo ordered Samarn, in Thai, to turn right at the next soi and stop at the rear entrance to the casino. Samarn did as he was ordered. Woo got out of the car and pressed a doorbell. The door was immediately opened by a tall, heavily built oriental. Tremayne thought him to be a Korean. The gunman ordered Tremayne and Samarn to get out of the car and enter the gloomy passage. Leading the way, Woo stopped at a door halfway down the passage and tapped on the door. There was the click of a key being turned in a lock and another tall Korean opened the door.

Tremayne and Samarn were pushed into the dimly lit room by the first Korean, and told to sit on a wooden form behind a trestle table.

Tremayne took the opportunity to survey the room while Woo and his gunman, who still held his pistol in his right hand, settled in comfortable cushion-filled rattan chairs, facing the trestle table. The two Koreans, who had produced US military carbines from a metal cupboard in the corner of the room, stood like sentries behind Tremayne and Samarn with their backs to the wall. The room was about fourteen feet square. It was windowless and sparsely furnished. There was a large earthenware water jug on a side table against the wall.

Tremayne's briefcase was propped against Woo's chair. Woo opened it and took out a packet of Rothmans. He selected one from the packet and lit it with a gold cigarette lighter. He tossed the packet to the young gunman, who took a cigarette out and lit it with a match scratched on the side of his chair.

Tremayne could have killed for a cigarette and the way things were developing, it looked as though he might have to do just that. 'Any chance of me having one of my cigarettes?' he asked.

Woo smiled as he puffed at the cigarette. 'First you must answer a few questions, group captain. If your answers are truthful I might let you have all your possessions back and let you return to your home. Firstly, what became of my emissary, the redoubtable Ming?'

'I told you in the car, he came to my house and told me that I owed you 138,000 baht. When I questioned the amount, he said that you had bought my IOUs. I had drawn the money out of my bank account in readiness to pay you and the other creditors, so I gave him the amount he asked for. He left my house at about ten o'clock carrying the money in a large brown paper bag. If he hasn't given you the money, he must have been tempted by such a large sum and gone on the run with it. Might have even crossed the border into Laos, or Cambodia.'

'Nice try, Group Captain, but I hardly think that he would go on the run in the nude!' He signalled the Korean next to the metal cupboard, who opened the door, pulled out a bulky sack and flung it on the table in front of Tremayne.

Tremayne was alarmed, but exercised control. 'What's this all about, Woo?' he sneered. 'I've not been frightened, or intimidated, by the unknown contents of sacks since I was about four years old, and found a sack of dead kittens at the bottom of my uncle's garden.'

Woo gave a hollow laugh. 'I grant you, Tremayne, you are a cool character under pressure, but let's stop pussyfooting. You know perfectly well what that sack contains—Ming's blood-stained clothing. The sack was found in the boot of your car, which we hijacked outside your home. Your driver did his utmost to thwart my men, but as most people would be, he was intimidated by having a pistol pressed against his head. He told me that he had seen the sack in the boot when he had been cleaning the car two days ago, but had not opened it. His words, "My master would be angry if I looked at things he wished to keep private." So, there's little doubt in my mind that you put the sack in the boot and that you have, somehow, managed to do away with one of my most loyal and resourceful employees. I should now like to hear your version of the event, particularly in relation to what became of the 138,000 baht you were supposed to have given Ming.'

'OK, I killed Ming. It was self-defence. He got nasty when I queried the amount I was supposed to owe you. I didn't believe that you had my other IOUs, and told him that I would only pay the 57,000 baht I owed you. He threatened me with his swordstick. I grabbed it and as we struggled he pulled at the scabbard end of the weapon, leaving me holding the blade. He then went for his gun and had cleared it from its holster. Believing I was about to be shot to death, I felt that I had every justification in defending myself. This I did, by stabbing him through his right eye with the swordstick. His death was almost instantaneous.'

Woo looked almost admiringly at Tremayne. 'You do tell a good story, group captain, but you've not explained what happened to the money. That's what I'm most interested in knowing about. I shan't even ask you what you've done with Ming's dead body. As good as he was, he can be easily replaced. But please tell me about the money. And no fairy tales this time.'

Tremayne's nerves were beginning to fray. 'Mr Woo, I'll tell you all about the money if you'll just let me have my cigarettes and brandy flask.'

Woo picked up the briefcase and looked inside. He saw the jumble of toiletries, the shaving kit, the hairbrush, the unopened carton of 200 cigarettes and three 20 packs of cigarettes, a chequebook and the brandy flask. He removed the shaving kit and took out the razor and nail scissors and threw them into the corner of the room. He closed the briefcase and threw it to Tremayne, who deftly caught it and placed it in front of him on the table. He opened the briefcase and took out a pack of cigarettes and the brandy flask. He lit a cigarette, opened the flask and took a long swig of the cognac. He returned the flask and cigarettes to the briefcase, but did not close it.

'Well, Group Captain Tremayne, I'm waiting. Tell me about the money.'

Tremayne cleared his throat. 'Well, as you know, I've been having a bad run of luck at the tables for several months now. More often losing than winning. So much so that I found myself owing a total of about 140,000 baht, to you and two other casino owners. But my luck suddenly changed when I recently visited a casino in Songkhla and won a considerable amount at the roulette table. I won more than enough to pay off you and my other two creditors. Of course, I don't keep such large sums at home so I banked it and it's there in my account at the Hong Kong and Shanghai Bank. So, if you will allow me to write you a cheque for the total I owe you, I'll be on my way.'

Woo's face became ugly. He raised his arm and made a signal to the Korean who was standing behind Tremayne. The Korean jabbed Tremayne sharply in the back with the butt of his carbine.

Tremayne winced with pain. What was wrong with his story, why didn't Woo believe him?

'I warned you Tremayne, I didn't want to hear any more of your fairy stories. I shall now give you the factual account. You did not leave the Lucky Chance Casino with a considerable amount of cash. In fact you lost your 5,000 baht stake money, along with the *considerable* amount of money you had won that evening. I should mention at this point that the owner of that casino is Mr Wun Cheung, a former business partner of mine. We casino owners might be competitors but we do keep in touch from time-to-time, to compare notes about big winners and even bigger losers, such as you, Tremayne. Because of the dilemma you were facing in having to pay your debts, a Miss Ruby Carterton, a wealthy Australian heiress, whom you had, shall we say, *befriended*, lent you 150,000 baht, which she had drawn from her account a day after your return from Songkhla. I must again digress to explain that one of my most useful informants is an under-manager at the Hong Kong and Shanghai Bank. He is a former customer of mine, who lost his savings and rather a lot of money he had secretly *borrowed* from the bank, at my casino. When I let him off the debt and repaid the money he had stolen from the bank, he became an unofficial employee of mine. But to continue with my story: two days after Miss Carterton had drawn that cash from the bank, Mrs Tremayne banked it in your joint account and then, inexplicably, immediately drew on this amount to pay for airline tickets and to send money to two people, presumably your children, in England and Switzerland. My latest information about your cash resources is that you have approximately 39,000 baht in your joint account. So, I ask myself, how are you going to pay me my 138,000 baht, or rather my 179,400 baht? I'm sorry, I forgot the daily increase of ten percent interest, to which the debt has been subject for the last three days.'

Tremayne raised his hands appealingly. 'It seems you have me over a barrel, Mr Woo, what can I do?'

'That's better, Tremayne, now you are facing realism. What would you say if I offered you a way out of your present difficulties? A way to pay off all your debts, recover your IOUs, and escape a possible murder charge?'

Tremayne half smiled. 'Sounds interesting; what do you want me to do, assassinate the Thai prime minister?'

Woo laughed. 'No, nothing like that. It's a much simpler task I have in mind for you. You have an aeroplane at your disposal, I believe.'

Tremayne thought, *what comes next*? 'Yes, I have a Devon, which is for my *official use* to fly to other capitals in the region, to which I am the accredited air attaché.'

'I notice you put an emphasis on the term *official use*, but I know differently. You have often taken your friends and relatives to places like Angkor Wat, Phnom Penh and Singapore. Anyway, what I want you to do is to pick up a consignment of goods from Laos. You are accredited to that country and have full diplomatic immunity. You can land at Vientiane without any undue formality. My representatives in that city would be there to meet you and load the aircraft. One of my men would travel with the cargo and when you returned to Bangkok, my men would meet your aircraft at Don Muang, where the cargo could be discharged and loaded onto your *Corps Diplomatique* plate bearing Landrover, driven, of course, by one of your staff and brought to this building.'

'You make it sound like a bit of a milk run,' said Tremayne with a forced laugh. 'But what cargo would I be carrying?'

'That need be no concern of yours,' snapped Woo. 'It's a take-it-or-leave offer. But if you decide to leave it, you must be prepared to take the consequences.'

'Just give me a minute to think it over while we all have a smoke,' said Tremayne as he rummaged in his briefcase with both hands. His left hand pulled out the two loose packs of cigarettes; these he threw to the Korean guards. They both reached down to pick up the cigarette packets without releasing their hold on their carbines. Tremayne's right hand came out of the briefcase holding Ming's Nambu automatic pistol. Tremayne fired left and right at the two Koreans, aiming at their arms that held their weapons. The Koreans screamed and dropped their carbines. The young Laotian gunman, who had been half dozing during Woo and Tremayne's discussion, suddenly came alive and raised his pistol to aim at Tremayne. Samarn shouted, 'Look front, master!' As the gunman fired wildly at them, Tremayne tipped the trestle table over and pulled Samarn down behind it. One of the gunman's wild shots hit Tremayne's Korean guard in the head, spattering his brains on the wall. Tremayne dived to one side and fired two shots at the gunman's chest. The man was dead before he hit the floor.

The wounded Korean was trying to fire his carbine with one hand. Samarn kicked his legs from under him. Then, snatching up the empty earthenware jug, he smashed it down on his head.

Woo, who was unarmed, had been watching the brief firefight in mute horror, and as Tremayne levelled his pistol at him, he raised his arms in surrender. 'Don't shoot, Tremayne, you win. All debts are cancelled. I'll give you a signed affidavit to that effect and return all your IOUs.'

'That's OK, I accept your offer, but just remember this, if you come up against me again I'll have no compunction about killing you.' Turning to Samarn: 'Collect all the weapons and ammo, put them in the car boot and start up the engine, Samarn, we're going home.'

'Yes, Master,' replied Samarn, as he quickly collected the two carbines and the automatic pistol from Woo's fallen henchmen.

Driving back, Tremayne turned to Samarn. 'You did well, Samarn. I shall reward you for your loyalty and bravery under fire. There's just one thing, though—you must promise me not to tell anyone of what happened tonight.'

Without taking his eyes off the road, Samarn said, 'I promise, master. I would die before I told anyone of tonight's happenings. But please tell me, master, how did you perform the magic with the gun in your briefcase. Why did Woo not see it when he searched the case?'

'Oh, that, Samarn, nothing magic about it. I had the gun hidden in a very useful compartment at the bottom of the case, which has been added to hide a camera. That's something else I don't want advertised.'

Samarn gave a rare smile. 'I understand, Master. No one shall learn from me of your magic with cameras and guns.'

CHAPTER 21

❀

Harry, Barry and Joe were back at their house for lunch, after an early morning send-off for the Commander-in-Chief, FEAF and his party and a wearying morning with Tremayne.

'Barry, you spend more time with the group captain than anybody else, so can you tell us what's eating him?' Harry said. 'He's always been a bit of a difficult-to-please taskmaster, but just recently he's become impossible!'

'You can say that again,' interposed Joe as he topped up his beer glass.

'Me, spend more time with him than anybody else? That's a big laugh!' retorted Barry. 'I'm in the office at seven every morning and I don't see him until about 8.30, and he's hardly ever in the office in the afternoons. He says he's attending meetings, but I'm never made aware of them until he's about to leave the office at lunchtime. It's my bet that while his wife is back in the UK he's carrying on with that Australian woman—Miss Carterton.'

'Can you blame him?' said Harry. 'His wife's just about over the hill and doesn't look as though there's a good shag left in her. But the Australian girl, now she's a real stunner—a bit of all right. I could do *big* things for her.'

'He's a bit old for her, isn't he? She can't be much more than 30 and he's 46,' said Joe, refilling his glass.

'Actually she's a bit older than she looks—probably about 35, and Tremayne lies about his age,' said Barry.

'Well, whatever age she is, she's certainly a tasty dish and I'd not kick her out of bed,' said Harry, with a lustful look in his eyes.

Barry laughed aloud. 'You'd not have the opportunity to kick her out of bed or, for that matter, do anything else with her. She's definitely "top drawer" in Australian society. She's not just a run-of-the-mill journo. Her father is a newspaper proprietor, and her mother left her oodles of lolly and a very desirable property. So, if she ever settles down, and somehow I can't see her doing that, she'll be looking for someone of a higher station than that of a master navigator—a group captain, perhaps.'

'Barry,' slurred Joe, 'what's a fucking journo?'

'Oh, journo, it's a new Australian slang word meaning journalist—you know, a writer of news reports.'

Harry suddenly banged his glass down and slopped orange juice over the table. 'I don't give a damn about the group captain's love life and, as far as I'm concerned, you can fuck all journos or journalists. You can hardly ever believe a word they write. I'm sure that when there's not much news to write about, they make up stories for their readers. What I want to know is how are we going to get our group captain in a better frame of mind?'

'We could throw a boozy do for him,' offered Joe, always ready to support such an event.

'That's a good idea,' agreed Barry. 'We could make it an RAF at-home evening. Invite some of the other air attachés and their staffs, and some of the former USAF guys, who now work for Air America; they're always good company and can spin some unbelievable yarns. Just one thing, though, do we make it a stag night, or shall we invite women—wives and escorts? If we have women guests it might help to keep the hangar doors closed. We don't want everybody talking shop all night.'

'Oh, yes, I agree, no talk of work, and we must have women,' said Harry, 'it wouldn't be a real party without them. They'll help brighten up the scene for the group captain—and us. Of course, it'll mean that we'll have to have some of those sponging bar hostesses and massage parlour girls here to partner up with the single and unaccompanied men. So, Barry, as we're all agreed, and as you know the form for organising this sort of thing, we'll leave it to you to send out invites to the right people, order the drinks from the embassy commissary, and get Noi to prepare one of her incomparable buffet suppers. You let us know what it all costs and Joe and I will pay our due. Let's see, it's Wednesday today. We could make it Saturday, that'll give those we invite just enough time to respond by phone.'

'OK, Harry, leave it to me. I'll see that it'll be a night to remember,' said Barry.

CHAPTER 22

❀

'Hello, Ruby, darling, I'm sorry I haven't been able to get down to the Oriental Hotel to see you during the last few days. I've had the new Commander-in-Chief FEAF up from Singapore, to make his courtesy calls. Thank heavens, he left yesterday and things will now get back to normal. I shan't be able to see you at all today, though. That's why I am phoning. I have so many things to catch up with. I'm glad I've had Barry to hold the fort for me; he's kept right on top of everything that really matters, but I have certain duties that I have to do myself. Is everything OK at your end?'

'Yes, Randy, everything is almost all right. But I am a little bored, being stuck in the hotel reading all day, or sitting outside on the terrace and watching ships sailing up and down the Chao Phraya River. Don't forget, I shall have to be on my way to Saigon early next week. I've already stayed longer in Bangkok than I had planned to do. And my father keeps sending me cables telling me to "get over to Saigon before the war ends". He's quite an optimist. I honestly believe it will go on for years. Even after the experience of the Korean War, the Americans and their SEATO supporters don't seem to have learnt much about the determination and fighting capabilities of the Asian Communists. Oh dear, just listen to me prattling on! You'd think I was sending in a story to my editor instead of talking to my lover. I do so look forward to your afternoon visits, so make every effort to get here tomorrow afternoon.'

'I shall, darling, I shall. Oh, I nearly forgot, Barry and the crew have organised an RAF at-home cocktail party at their house and we've been invited, along with an assortment of American types. It's on Saturday—would you like to go? I'll have to attend, because I suspect that it is for me they are doing it. Barry has told me several times that I don't look very well and that I am in need of a little rest and recreation. He thinks that my attending all these *official meetings* is tiring me out—little does he know the real cause of my tired looks, darling.'

'I'd love to go to their party. It sounds as though it might be fun. I rather like Barry, he seems a *useful* sort of chap and Joe is the salt of the earth. But I'm afraid I'm not too keen on your navigator. He strikes me as being a bit of a dirty old man.'

'Pay no heed to Harry, he's really quite harmless. He talks a lot about sex, but when it comes right down to it, I suspect that it is just *talk* with him. Anyway, I'm glad you want to go their party. Of course, it'll certainly be a little different to the usual embassy cocktail parties, but their cook does a splendid buffet and the boys spare no expense over the drinks. I'll say cheerio now—until tomorrow, darling.'

'Goodbye, Randy, I look forward to seeing you tomorrow. I'll try to be *gentle* with you. I wouldn't want you to look too washed out for the party.'

CHAPTER 23

Han Woo sat at his office desk in the Lucky Strike Casino. He was worried. The strategy that he had planned to secure the use of an aeroplane, piloted by a man with diplomatic immunity, had failed. He was disappointed and he knew that the man he was about to telephone would be equally, if not more, disappointed at his failure. The man was powerful in Laos and wealthy beyond belief. He was utterly ruthless and intolerant of failure—a man who could, because of his wide circle of contacts throughout the world, exact swift and violent vengeance upon anyone, wherever they chose to hide or flee, to escape his wrath.

Woo looked across the room at one of his few remaining bodyguards, a Korean giant with his head swathed in bandages and his right arm in a sling. He had a Smith and Wesson, .38 calibre revolver stuck in his belt on his right side. He was reading an American comic, the one that came as a weekly supplement with the *Bangkok World*. Woo sighed deeply and shook his head. This man could never replace Ming. He'd been a man who would die for his employer, and had. What he now needed were some more men like Ming before he made another move against that surprisingly resourceful airman diplomat.

'Leave me, Daeng, and return when I call you.'

Daeng folded up his comic, tucked it into his sling and walked out of the office to sit in a chair outside in the passage to continue reading about the exploits of Superman.

Woo picked up his telephone. His right hand was shaking so much that he had difficulty in dialling the number he wanted. There was a 10 second delay before the telephone was answered.

'Hello, who speaks?'

'It is Han Woo. May I speak with Mr George Lloyd, please?'

'First you must identify yourself. What is your code name?'

Woo thought for a few seconds, 'It is Lyndon Baines Johnson,' he replied, smiling to himself over George's twisted sense of humour in choosing that name for him.

The voice was satisfied. 'Please wait, Mr George is engaged elsewhere. He will speak to you as soon as he is free.'

Woo lit a cigarette and waited, for ten minutes or more, his nervousness returning. He tried to think of something to say that might please George. Nothing came to mind. He'd just have to take his chances with George.

'Hello, Woo, I was beginning to wonder when I might hear from you. I hope that you have good news for me. My cargo is ready for delivery.'

'Well…er…not exactly. There have been a few problems, but I hope to proceed as was planned within the next few days.'

'What you say bothers me. Especially when you were so confident that it was just a matter of rigging a few roulette wheels to entrap our man. But please don't burden me with your excuses, just tell me what is needed to get the plan back on track or, perhaps I should say, a plane in the air.'

Woo felt slightly relieved. He had not wanted to have to tell George Lloyd all the details about Tremayne's resourceful thwarting of his purpose. Better to keep it simple. 'I have had a permanent loss of manpower and need more men at this end to ensure everything goes as it should.'

'You've had a permanent loss of manpower? Do you mean to tell me that Tremayne has actually killed some of your men? You're not supposed to be engaging in some sort of shooting match with him. Tremayne would be no use to us dead! What you need to get this man to work for us is not force, but guile—use it. Find a means of putting extreme pressure on him, or make him an offer he can't refuse. As regards your need for reinforcements, I shall send a team of four of my best men. They will be with you tomorrow. As they will be flying in on a commercial airline they will not be carrying weapons. I leave you to see that they are provided as necessary. Use my men well, and remember if you should fail me again I shall be obliged to make other arrangements that might not be favourable to you. Goodbye, Woo. I shall expect to hear from you very soon.'

'Please be assured, Mr Lloyd, I shall not fail you again.'

Woo replaced the phone and dried his sweating palms with a handkerchief, lit a cigarette and called Daeng back into the office. 'Put that comic away and listen to me, Daeng. I want Tremayne followed everywhere he goes and I want to know whom he meets. But that's not a job for you. You're as obvious as The Grand Palace. Get a couple of reliable men on the job straight away.'

'OK, Mr Woo, I'll see to that for you,' said Daeng, slouching out of the office.

CHAPTER 24

❈

'Good evening, sir, good evening, Miss Carterton,' welcomed Barry, acting host for the party. 'I'm so pleased that you were *both* able attend our little informal gathering.'

Tremayne looked troubled, but grinned. 'Good evening, Barry. Looks as though you've turned over a few stones to get this lot together tonight.'

'Yes, sir, but they are all flyers, or ex-aircrew types. Most of whom I feel sure, you'll know.'

Tremayne nodded and continued surveying the gathered guests.

'Good evening, Barry, and thank you so much for inviting me,' said Ruby, touching Barry's arm. 'Bangkok can be such a lonely city for a young woman on her own. It's no fun sitting in a hotel all night watching American programmes like *Bonanza*, *Combat* and *Coronation Street*, dubbed in Thai.'

Barry laughed. 'I know exactly what you mean about the television programmes. That giant cowboy Hoss Cartwright dubbed by a Thai voice is the funniest thing on television. Our servants can't understand it when we all laugh at the serious scenes. But you can get the original American sound track on FM radio, to play, with the television soundtrack turned off.' Barry noticed Tremayne's impatient look—he wanted a drink. 'But enough about television, I feel I am neglecting you. What will you have to drink, Miss Carterton?'

'Barry, this is an informal affair, so less of the *Miss Carterton!* My name is *Ruby*, to you, and I'd love a Mai Tai, or is that too exotic for your bar?'

'No, that's a drink we *can* provide. We have a Hawaiian friend who gets it from the PX for us. I know what you'll want, sir—Remy Martin. We've got a bottle in specially for you.'

'Splendid, so be a good chap and get me a large one, as soon as you can.'

Barry passed their drinks order to Joe who was in his element as barman and waiter for the evening.

Barry excused himself and joined the group of American enlisted men, who were gathered around Lieutenant Colonel Bradford Rantzen, newly returned from the USA after his wife's funeral. Rantzen was no snob and was not overly conscious of his social position when he was in the company of junior officers and non-commissioned officers. That had made him very popular with the rank and file when he had commanded flying units, but his liberal mindedness didn't go down too well with his superiors.

Rantzen hadn't wanted to attend the party, but Colonel Merkle had insisted that he did. 'I can't go, Brad, I've got much more important engagements this weekend, dinner with the ambassador for one thing. But it'll do you good; get you back in the swing of things.' Rantzen was now glad that he had come and was enjoying yarning with the embassy aircrew and some of the Air America personnel.

Tremayne introduced Ruby to Dan Murtagh, a retired USAF lieutenant colonel, who ran Air America's Bangkok office. 'Now here's someone with plenty of exclusive news, but it'll take all of your feminine wiles to get anything out of him,' said Tremayne with undisguised cynicism.

'Oh, Air America, the CIA's *private* air force,' exclaimed Ruby, her eyes gleaming. 'I'm sure an interview with you, Dan, would result in some highly informative copy that would gladden the heart of any editor.'

Murtagh gave her an admiring look. 'Well, a girl like you might just be able to get me to let down my guard long enough to give you the low down on some of our very necessary, but often considered heavy-handed, undercover tactics in the cause of saving the Far East, if not the Free World, from Communism.'

'Tell me Dan,' asked Ruby with a wicked glint in her eyes, 'do you really drop sacks of rice all over Laos, or is it just bombs that you deliver?'

Murtagh looked startled, but smiled thinly. 'I guess it could be a mixture of both. The sacks of rice are dropped, primarily, to feed the families of the Hmong tribesmen who are away from their villages fighting the Communist Pathet Lao forces. We also supply them with arms. There's about 10,000 Hmong tribesmen fighting the Communists, and they're great little fighters. If there are any bombs dropped, they'd be for the Pathet Lao.'

'Thank you, Dan, what you had to say was most interesting. I must drop by your office one day, when, perhaps, you'll allow me to interview you for my newspaper—*The Sydney Star.*'

'I've never heard of your paper, but you're welcome to come to my office anytime!'

Time to move along, thought a jealous Tremayne, as he eased Ruby away from Murtagh. Out of earshot: 'That horny old Texan was trying to get fresh with you.'

Ruby laughed. 'Fresh? What—that crumbly old colonel? I'd say he's well past his useful best in bed.'

Tremayne covertly grabbed her hand and squeezed it. 'You were playing him along a bit just to make me jealous, weren't you?'

'Of course, Randy, you're all the man I want. Let's go and talk to Brad Rantzen and find out how things are with him now that he's back.'

Tremayne and Rantzen shook hands, and Rantzen kissed Ruby's cheek.

I'd better not mention the funeral; he'll probably not want to talk about it yet, thought Tremayne. 'It's good to see you back, Brad. How is your daughter?'

'Oh, she's fine, she's at last getting over the loss of her baby, but like all the family, she's still grieving over the death of her mother,' replied Rantzen, with sadness reflected in his eyes.

'Has your son rejoined his unit yet?' asked Tremayne, for something else to say.

'Yeah, his CO didn't waste much time about getting him back into action. Ben sent me an encrypted message via our embassy in Saigon and here. He said he was doing fighting patrols west of Khe Sanh, right up to the Laos border. Not the safest area in Vietnam at this time, but Ben's a good soldier and he's doing what he's paid for. Perhaps it was the best thing he could do, getting straight back into action. There's nothing like combat to sharpen your mind and focus your attention on nothing else but the job in hand and staying alive.'

'You've made a good point there, Brad, I couldn't agree more,' said Tremayne, and meant it.

As is the customary practice at embassy cocktail parties, Tremayne and Ruby continued to circulate and talk to as many people as possible. Ruby, thinking it would look better and stop tongues wagging if she spent more time on her own, left Tremayne's side to chat with some of the US Defence Attaché's staff.

'Hi guys, I'm Ruby Carterton, an Australian journo at large. Have you anything worth printing in *The Sydney Star*?'

'Yes, Mam, I certainly have. You can thank your folks back home for the support the Anzacs are giving us in Vietnam. There may not be many of them, but we sure as hell appreciate their company. You can quote me, Technical Sergeant Carl Mellors of the United States Air Force.'

'Why thank you, Sergeant Mellors, I shall be pleased to pass on your appreciation.'

'Well, I'd like to personally show my appreciation to an Australian, so how about you, baby,' said CPO Andy Sanders, who had drunk more than his limit of Joe Swaine's 'extra special' cocktails and was reaching out to take hold of Ruby.

Barry was suddenly beside them. 'Don't go overboard, sailor. We're all having a great time; so don't spoil it by getting too familiar with our lady guests.'

'No offence intended madam, or to you, my Royal Air Force friend,' Andy slurred as he staggered back to the bar to talk Joe into making him "one for the road".

Tremayne joined Ruby and Barry, who were deeply engrossed in a lively discussion with Captain Michael Denver, the US Air Attache's navigator, and Harry Simmons, about the feasibility of landing a manned spacecraft on the moon.

'Would you like me to escort you back to your hotel, Miss Carterton?' asked Tremayne, in as loud a voice for most around to hear. 'I haven't got my car tonight, but we'll not have to wait long for a taxi; they're always thick on the ground at night.'

'Yes, please, Group Captain, I should be most grateful if you would. I wouldn't fancy having to take a taxi ride on my *own* in Bangkok, so late at night.'

'Goodnights' were exchanged and Tremayne and Ruby left.

The senior guest having left, the remainder of the guests quickly dispersed, leaving Harry, Joe and Barry, with their three Thai female 'escorts' for the evening. Joe suggested a *special* cocktail nightcap and a nice tepid shower to freshen up before they all went to bed. Nobody raised an objection.

CHAPTER 25

'Come in,' answered Lieutenant Colonel Bradford Rantzen to the light knock on his door. Rantzen pushed aside the documents he was reading as Colonel Merkle and an unknown army major stepped into the office.

Rantzen rose from his chair. 'Good morning, colonel, good morning, major.'

Who is this guy? thought Rantzen, *and what's going on? Merkle never comes to my office; he always sends for me if he wants to discuss anything or issue instructions to me.*

Merkle looked ill at ease. 'Brad, this officer is Major Drobnick of the 2nd Battalion, First Cavalry Division.'

Rantzen, looked startled. 'That's Ben's outfit. What's this all about? You're not here to tell me that Ben has been killed or wounded, are you?'

Merkle and Drobnick exchanged questioning glances.

'Brad, Major Drobnick is over here on business with the JUS-MAG people. His battalion commander asked him to come to see you, before he did anything else, to give you a first-hand report about your son, Lieutenant Ben Rantzen, he—'

'Oh, for God's sake, major,' Rantzen interrupted, 'what's happened to my son? Is he dead or wounded?'

'As far as we have been able to ascertain we believe that he is alive and unwounded. But he has been captured by Pathet Lao irregulars,' answered Drobnick, with relief in his voice.

'Captured by the Pathet Lao? How the hell did that happen in South Vietnam?' Rantzen angrily questioned.

'Brad, let's all sit down and have coffee and Major Drobnick will give you a report on all he knows of the incident,' said Merkle. Then, opening Rantzen's door, he called, 'Andy, organize some coffee for three in here, soonest, please.'

Merkle and Drobnick settled in the visitors' armchairs. Barely a minute passed before a young Thai woman brought in a tray loaded with a coffee pot, three cups and saucers, cream, sugar and a plate of cookies. She served the three officers and quickly left the room.

'The floor is yours, major, please tell Brad all you know about his son's capture.'

Drobnick cleared his throat. 'Lieutenant Ben Rantzen was detailed to take his platoon on a reconnaissance patrol to an area several miles north-west of Khe Sanh, where our chopper patrols had seen signs of a North Vietnamese Army build up in preparation, it was thought, for a major attack on Khe Sanh. Lieutenant Rantzen was in radio communication with battalion headquarters and reported that his platoon had found no traces of any significant troop movements in the area. He was ordered to move westward to reconnoitre along the Laos border. His next message to battalion was that his unit had come under heavy attack by a company size force of what he believed were Pathet Lao irregular troops. As his mission was one of reconnaissance, his men were not carrying heavy weapons, and he had been instructed to get in and out of the area as quickly as possible. It soon became evident that his unit could not hold out long against the larger and more heavily armed force. His radioman was killed and his radio put out of action. He then ordered his platoon sergeant, Sergeant First Class Raul McLeish, to break out with three of the platoon's squads, before they were entirely encircled and to get back to our lines as best they could. Your son stayed behind with his remaining squad to cover McLeish's retreat.' Drobnick paused to drink some coffee.

'Major, never mind the damned coffee, go on, what happened, how do you know Ben was captured?' cried Rantzen in a voice wracked with anguish.

Drobnick looked hurt, but went on. 'When McLeish and the survivors of the platoon reached our lines a flight of choppers was sent out to support the trapped unit, but when a squad was landed to check the position, they found about eight or nine of our guys dead and stripped of their weapons. Apart from your son, the only member of the squad not immediately accounted for was a PFC Dunn. He was later found hiding in heavy shrub. He'd been badly wounded, but had managed to crawl away to safety before the squad was completely overrun. He told us how the guerrillas had finished off the wounded men, and captured Lieutenant Rantzen. He said he felt sure that he had been unwounded when taken away by the guerrillas. He also said that about 25 dead and wounded guerrillas had been removed from the area.

'What does all this mean? I can't understand why they didn't kill Ben like the rest of his men?' said Rantzen.

'Because your son was unwounded, he was probably kept alive to be exchanged for a bounty paid by the North Vietnamese Army for the capture of US officers and senior non-coms, who they think might have useful military intelligence to impart under interrogation. Or, who could be brainwashed for propaganda purposes,' explained Drobnick.

Rantzen paled and his stomach churned. Interrogation, brainwashing—he knew all about that from his time in the North

Korean POW camp. 'You mean like the gooks did to our men in the Korean War?'

'Gooks?' Queried Drobnick.

'Yes, gooks! That's what we called the North Koreans, and isn't that what our troops are now calling the North Vietnamese?' shouted Rantzen.

'Yes, I imagine so,' answered Drobnick. 'But once your son has been handed over to the North Vietnamese Army for questioning and they find that he has little or nothing of value to tell, apart from his number, rank and name, in accordance with the Geneva Convention, they'll probably just cage him up with all the other prisoners of ours they have.'

'*Geneva Convention*! Those Communist sons-of-bitches don't give a shit about that, or any other convention, they'll—'

'Steady, Brad, things may not be half as bad as you imagine,' said Merkle in his quiet voice.

'Yes, Colonel Rantzen, and although it might not be of much consolation to you at this time, I am to tell you that my battalion commander has taken into consideration the statements of Sergeant First Class McLeish and Private First Class Dunn, which were supported by the officer who led the search of the area where the action took place, and is preparing a citation recommending your son, Lieutenant Ben Rantzen for the award of a silver star for gallantry. The battalion commander is convinced that had it not been for your son's gallant rearguard action, Sergeant McLeish and the surviving men of the platoon would have all been killed or captured.'

'Now, Brad, there's nothing any of us can do for Ben. We must just wait and hope that no harm comes to him. In the meantime I want you to go home to your apartment and stay there for a few days. Try to come to terms with the situation, and try to be comforted by the fact that everything is being done by the Red

Cross to ensure that all prisoners of war are being fairly treated and not being subjected to the sort of thing that went on in Communist run PoW camps in the Korean War.'

Rantzen ignored Merkle's appeal. What did he know about what went on in PoW camps? You had to have been in one to know that. He turned to Drobnick and tried to smile, but it wouldn't come. He stretched out his hand to Drobnick. 'Thank you, major, for your detailed verbal report, and please tell your battalion commander that I was proud to learn that Ben is likely to receive recognition for his bravery. Please let me know if you hear of anything else concerning my son.'

'Of course, I will, colonel,' said Drobnick, as he shook Rantzen's hand.

🍁 🍁 🍁

Rantzen sat in his cane chair with a bottle of Jack Daniels on the side table at his right elbow. He reached over to refill his glass. His hand was shaking; surely not with just three fingers of Jack Daniels, he thought. No, of course, it wasn't that. He was thinking of what was happening to Ben.

His housekeeper, Suporn, approached him with her head lowered. 'Master not want nice runch I make special for you?'

She was a treasure; she'd looked after him well when Nora had been in the Stateside hospital and now she was doing her utmost to please him in every way she could. She was a widow with two young children. Her husband was one of the first casualties suffered by the Thai Army, when they had joined in the fight against the North Vietnamese Army and Viet Cong.

'No, thank you, Suporn, I'm not hungry for food. You take it for your children.'

'Thank you, master,' she said as she bowed and walked backwards out of the room. Rantzen had tried to get her to drop the Thai culture of servants and those of the lower classes always keeping themselves below their employers, masters and any others they might consider held higher status than themselves. But she had made the point that should she leave his employ, or that of any other American—they can't be staying in Thailand for ever, she reasoned—she would have to work in a similar capacity for a middle or upper class Thai, most of whom would insist that the traditional master-servant relationship was strictly observed at all times.

Rantzen sipped his Jack Daniels, and closed his eyes to try to visualize the time when he had a whole family: a devoted wife and mother, now dead; a loving, but headstrong daughter, who had married earlier than he would have wished, miscarried her baby son, and as a result was told she'd not be able to bear another child; a son who showed much promise in college, and could have gone on to become a doctor or a lawyer, but wanted to follow the family tradition—a career in the military, but not the air force, like his father. He chose the army like his grandfather, who had been killed in the Argonne Forest. Leaving his only child, Bradford, fatherless at just three years old. Now Ben was being held a captive of God knows whom. *I'd give my eyes to free him.* Brad's thoughts meandered as he slowly drifted off to sleep.

🍁   🍁   🍁

'Shall I kill him, comrade lieutenant?' asked the brutish looking Korean soldier, his bayonet pointing at the American airman who had just fallen from the sky and was struggling to free himself from his parachute harness.

'No, take his pistol and secure him. He is an officer and might be a valuable prisoner.'

The brutish soldier pulled the airman's .45 Colt automatic pistol from its shoulder holster and handed it to the lieutenant, who thrust it behind his tunic belt.

The rest of the Korean officer's men crowded around the airman and pulled off his parachute, and tied his hands behind his back. They tried to pull the airman to his feet, but his left ankle had been badly broken in landing awkwardly on the rocky ridge.

The officer who had been to University and could speak several languages spoke to him in English. 'What nationality are you, American?'

'Yes, American, you slant-eyed gook!'

The Korean officer struck the airman's face with the back of his hand. 'Show more respect to your captor. What is your name?'

'My name is Bradford Ralph Rantzen, lieutenant colonel USAF, number O-2-3-8-7-9-4, and that's all you're going to get from me, knuckle-head.'

The Korean officer hit Rantzen on the side of his face with his clenched fist. 'What is the name of your unit, colonel?'

'Barnum and Bailey's Flying Circus!'

'Very well, colonel, if you wish to make a joke of your situation, that's entirely up to you; but when I hand you over to our intelligence officers for questioning you would do well to be more cooperative. They're far better skilled at questioning prisoners than I am, and they are completely without the sort of sense of humour that would laugh at your stupid and unfunny American jokes.'

'Well, Lieutenant Gook, if you want to take me anywhere you'll have to carry me on a litter. If you don't want to do that you'd better shoot me now, because I know I couldn't get off this ridge unaided and I don't fancy lying around up here when night falls and the temperature drops to freezing.'

The Korean lieutenant called his sergeant over. 'Detail some men to find some timber to make a litter for this prisoner. Two thin trees, or saplings, strung together with rope or rifle slings should do the job.'

'Is it your wish, comrade lieutenant, that this man be carried down to the valley and on to our base? I would advise against this. It is dangerous and will slow us down to a crawling pace, and if there are any more enemy aircraft about we would be an easy target for them,' the sergeant demurred.

'Comrade sergeant, I am aware that you have been in the army much longer than me and that you fought the Japanese in the World War and that you were awarded a medal for bravery in the fighting to repel the American invaders at Inchon, but I am your superior officer and am ordering you to make a litter. This man is a senior officer and will possess much useful information for our intelligence officers. Now do as I ask, or I shall put you on report when we get back to base.'

'Very well, comrade lieutenant, I shall attend to the matter straight away. But I request that you place on record that I drew your attention to the possible dangers of taking this decision, and advised against this course of action.'

The lieutenant nodded agreement, and the sergeant immediately shouted instructions to his men to find the necessary materials and make the litter.

In spite of the pain he was suffering, Rantzen couldn't help smiling when he thought of how Communism was affecting the long established and deeply entrenched autocracy in the military, between those who gave orders and those who were expected to follow them without question.

A makeshift litter was made. Rantzen was tied to it and carefully carried down from the ridge and into the valley where the lieutenant's unit was based.

When the party arrived, the lieutenant instructed the litter bearers to take Rantzen to the base first aid post for attention to be given to his broken ankle. An elderly medical officer and a young corporal male nurse set Rantzen's broken ankle without the aid of anaesthetic. Rantzen felt agonising pain, as the medical officer manipulated the broken anklebones into place. But Rantzen was determined to deny his captors the satisfaction of seeing him give way to his suffering and bit on his leather holster strap until it parted and then, mercifully, slipped into unconsciousness.

When Rantzen came around he was lying on a stretcher, in a wooden hut. His flying suit had been removed and was laid over the back of a ramshackle chair next to the stretcher. He looked at his left wrist for the time, but his watch had been removed. He guessed, from the position of the sun that shone through the open door of the hut, that it was a little past midday. He must have been unconscious, or asleep for 24 hours. He looked down at his left ankle, and saw that it was tightly bandaged. The pain in his ankle was excruciating, but his thirst concerned him most. He tried to call out but could only croak: 'Water, water, please give me water.' Almost immediately, the male nurse appeared, carrying a large metal jug and a tin cup. He poured water into the cup and handed it to Rantzen, who quickly drank the water and held out the cup for more. The nurse refilled the cup, set the jug down beside the stretcher and turned to leave the room, without having said a word.

'Do you speak English?' croaked Rantzen.

The nurse turned and moved to the end of the stretcher. 'Yes, I speak a little. I learnt at school.'

'Please tell me what is happening to me.'

The nurse looked sympathetic and answered in almost a whisper. 'You are to be taken to our divisional headquarters tomorrow morning. That is where many Americans are held prisoner. I shall now bring you some rice and fish to eat. When you have eaten you should sleep. We have no drugs to take away your pain, so sleep is the best thing to do and your bones will heal better if you do not move your leg.'

Rantzen whispered, 'Thank you,' as the nurse left the room.

🍁   🍁   🍁

When Rantzen awoke in a lightless room, dressed only in his underpants and vest, he was sitting in a chair with his body tied in such a way that he could not move his shoulders or his head. Only his left foot was not bound, but wrapped in what looked like pieces of sacking. His foot felt numb and his whole body ached as though he had been in one position too long. Suddenly, he felt a splash of water on his forehead, then another and another. Rantzen timed the space between the drips: 1-20, 2-20, 3.20, 4.20, 5.20 drip. The drips were timed to hit his head every five seconds. At first he felt refreshed by the water hitting his forehead and lightly splashing his cheeks, but after what he calculated to be two hours, the drips began to feel as though they were hammers hitting his head. Suddenly, the dripping stopped and bright lights blinded him. The door he faced across the room was flung open and two men walked in and stopped in front of him.

The men were dressed in Korean Army uniform and he could see by their badges of rank that the younger and slightly built of the two was a captain and his companion, a burly man of nearly six feet tall, was a sergeant. The captain was carrying a clipboard with papers attached. The sergeant carried a leather attaché case.

The captain spoke. 'I am Homnit Ragoon, a captain in the North Korean Intelligence Corps and my colleague is Sergeant Jabob Nguyen, also of the Korean Army Intelligence Corps. I speak and understand English very well. My comrade sergeant understands English, but does not speak it well enough to hold a conversation. So I shall do all the questioning.

'What is your name?'

Rantzen thought, *how do I play this, should I see how much they are prepared to put up with before they turn nasty? I'll give it a go.* 'John Wayne,' he replied.

'John Wayne?' The captain looked puzzled, and looked at his clipboard. 'The officer who captured you and took your personal details has recorded your name as "Bradford Ralph Rantzen", and the documents you were carrying confirm that is your name.'

'If you know all that, why the hell are you wasting time asking me?'

The captain's face was expressionless. 'We have our methods and these are carried out to ascertain the degree of cooperation we may expect from you. We shall start again. And this time I do not want to hear any foolish answers. What is your name?'

Out of the corner of his eye Rantzen could see the sergeant undoing his leather case and knew that he had to play ball, or they *would* turn nasty.

'Bradford Ralph Rantzen.'

'What is your service number?'

'O-2-3-8-7-9-4.'

'Good, that is correct. Now what is your rank?'

'Lieutenant colonel, and under the terms of the Geneva Convention, I'm not obliged to give you any further information.'

The captain's eyes narrowed until they were hardly visible, but he ignored Rantzen's remark. 'What is the title and location of your unit?'

'Teddy Roosevelt's Rough Riders, based in San Antonio, Texas.'

The captain nodded to the sergeant, who produced a two-foot length of thin rubber hose. He hit Rantzen across his right shoulder. Rantzen winced at the stinging pain, but made no sound.

'Where is your unit located and how many of your aircraft are serviceable and available for operations?' continued the captain in the same mild manner.

'My service number is O-2-3-8-7-9-4, my rank is lieutenant colonel and my name is Bradford Ralph Rantzen.'

The captain nodded to the sergeant, who hit Rantzen's left shoulder with the rubber hose. Again the stinging pain made Rantzen wince, but he made no sound.

'You are being foolish, colonel. You *will* tell us what we wish to know, or things will become even more unpleasant for you,' the captain said, as though he were a headmaster, brandishing a bamboo cane as he addressed a disobedient schoolboy in his study.

'Go stick your head up your ass, you sadistic, slant-eyed gook!'

The captain nodded to the sergeant and pointed to Rantzen's broken ankle. The sergeant swung the rubber hose high and brought it down with vicious force upon the ankle. Rantzen gave a short sharp scream and fainted.

'Sergeant, revive him with a bucket of cold water and leave him to consider his position.'

The sergeant went to the door and shouted to a soldier to fetch a bucket of water. The sergeant grabbed the bucket from the soldier and hurled the contents of the bucket straight at Rantzen's face. Rantzen came to, but feigned unconsciousness. The captain and the sergeant left the room.

It was about an hour later that the captain and the sergeant returned to the room. The sergeant untied Rantzen from the chair, made him stand up and tied his wrists to two iron rings fixed into the wall. He adjusted the cords so that Rantzen's right wrist was tied higher than his left. This brought Rantzen's right foot off the floor and lowered his left foot to the floor, to bear the weight of his body on his fractured ankle. Rantzen could do nothing to relieve the excruciating agony. But worse was to come. The sergeant produced two electrical cattle prods and applied them to his left leg. The surge of current made his leg jerk off the floor and each time it dropped to hit the floor, a wave of agonising pain shot up Rantzen's leg. He drifted in and out of consciousness. During his moments of consciousness he could hear the now muffled voice of the captain. 'Where is your unit located and how many…' The voice faded away and he once more drifted into merciful unconsciousness

🍁 🍁 🍁

'Master, master, your dinner is leddy.'

It was the voice of Suporn that Rantzen heard, as he awoke from his recurring nightmare. His body was bathed in sweat and there was a dull pain in his left foot. 'Thank you, Suporn; I'll have it later. Now I must have a drink of water first, and then a large Jack Daniels,' said Rantzen, as he poured bourbon into his glass and Suporn ran to the kitchen to fetch ice cold water.

CHAPTER 26

❀

'Have you any success to report to me, Daeng?' asked Woo.

'Yes, I have, Mr Woo,' said the ugly, giant Korean. His right arm was still in a sling, but his head was unbandaged and covered by a baseball cap. 'My men have followed Group Captain Tremayne and report that he has been meeting with a young woman called Ruby Carterton, an Australian journalist, who is staying at the Oriental Hotel. She sits out on the rear terrace, overlooking the river each morning smoking cigarettes, drinking coffee, making notes in a notebook and reads a Sydney newspaper. Tremayne goes to the hotel after lunch each day and stays with her in her room most of the afternoon. My men have spoken to members of the hotel staff, who confirm that this is so. They have taken food and beverages to the room and found Tremayne and the woman in dressing gowns. The headwaiter, who, I believe, has been a heavy loser on your tables and owes you much money, has told me that this woman is very, very wealthy and that her father is the owner and publisher of an Australian newspaper. From snatches of their conversation overheard by waiters it seems that the Carterton woman is soon to go to Saigon.'

Woo beamed at his henchman. 'You have done well, Daeng. The news you bring must be told to George Lloyd in Vientiane. Tell me, are the four men that Mr Lloyd sent to help us, still staying at the Imperial Hotel?'

'Yes, Mr Woo, they sit and play cards and watch television all day, awaiting your instructions.'

'Fine, then I want you to arrange to provide them with weapons, that may be easily concealed about their person. We have several .38 calibre Browning automatic pistols in our armoury, and plenty of spare magazines. Issue them with those. Tell them to remain on the alert for immediate action when they get a message from me.'

'Is there anything else, before I go, Mr. Woo?'

'Just one thing, Daeng, check that our cabin cruiser moored at Klong Toey is serviceable for immediate use and have it refuelled.'

'I'm off then, Mr Woo, goodbye.'

'Goodbye, Daeng.'

Woo, a self-satisfied look on his face, sat still in his chair, arched his fingers and patted them together as he thought about what he had to tell Mr Lloyd. Things were going well. Even Daeng was beginning to show initiative. But best of all, Tremayne was slowly embroiling himself in a situation that would put him completely under their control. Time to update George Lloyd. Woo dialled the Vientiane number. Lloyd's receptionist answered the phone immediately.

'Hello, who is there?'

'It is Han Woo and I wish to speak with Mr George Lloyd.'

'What is your codename?'

'Lyndon Baines Johnson.'

'Please wait, Woo.'

Expecting a long wait, Woo lit a cigarette. But barely a minute had passed before George Lloyd came on the line.

'I'm glad you have telephoned, Woo; I was beginning to get impatient. I expected a call from you much sooner. Everything is ready at this end, the poppies were harvested right on time, the opium was quickly produced and has been processed into freebase cocaine and heroin and packaged to the specifications you gave me for transportation. I gave priority to this work, expecting you would come up with the necessary transport arrangements much sooner. What is the current position?'

Woo sat back in his chair and savoured the moment. 'Mr Lloyd, all is well, please relax and listen to my plan.' Woo spoke at length, without any interruption or response from Lloyd until he had finished.

'I like your plan, Woo. If it goes down as well as you have explained to me, I shall make you a very rich man. I look forward to the arrival of your aeroplane. When its ETA has been decided telephone this office.'

'Leave it to me, Mr Lloyd; everything will go as I have planned.'

'Don't hang up yet, Woo, I wish to tell you of some very interesting news I have received from one of my Bangkok agents, a Thai woman who works as a catering assistant in the American Embassy. My agent tells me that Pathet Lao forces near the border with Thailand have captured the soldier son of Lieutenant Colonel Rantzen, who is the US assistant air attaché, and is, of course, a pilot. His son is an infantry lieutenant and the Pathet Lao will probably want to hand him over to the North Vietnamese Army for the bounty they pay for American officers. I understand that they brainwash them and use them for propaganda purposes. But I have already been in contact with the Pathet Lao high command and made them an offer of whatever they want: money, weapons, explosives or drugs in exchange for Lieutenant Rantzen. They have agreed and have promised to transfer the young officer to my custody within the next day or two. As the Americans would say, Woo, "How about them apples?"'

'I'm afraid you lost me there, Mr Lloyd. They don't grow apples in Thailand, and I'm unfamiliar with the phrase. And I don't understand how you propose to make any use of Lieutenant Rantzen.'

Lloyd laughed. 'Your education in things American is a little lacking, but no matter. With regard to the use that can be made of Lieutenant Rantzen, you, as a gambler, should know that in the poker game of life, it is better to have two aces in the hole rather than just one. Goodbye, Woo and keep in touch.'

CHAPTER 27

❀

Tremayne's head appeared around the door of his office. 'Barry,' he called in a near whisper, barely audible above the clatter of Barry's now ancient Imperial war finish typewriter, 'please come in.'

Barry stopped typing, picked up his notebook and pencils and entered Tremayne's office and stood in front of his desk.

'Sit yourself down here, Barry,' Tremayne invited, pointing to the easy chair usually reserved for VIP guests. 'Are the other assistants around this morning?'

'No, sir, everybody is out. Colonel Purvis has taken Diana with him to the SEATO meeting and Hughes is down at the docks with Commander Lancaster.'

Tremayne looked pleased. 'That's good, we'll not be disturbed then—well, at least, not by the Defence Staff. What I have to tell you is in the strictest confidence. I don't want you to breathe a word to anybody else about what I am about to tell you.'

Tremayne looked hard at Barry, presumably expecting an assurance that he would 'keep mum' about what he was to divulge.

'I understand, sir. It's my job to keep secrets, and I do hold an almost top level security clearance, so you can trust me with whatever military secrets you pass on to me.'

Tremayne frowned. 'Well, what I have to confide to you are not actually military secrets, they are rather more of a personal nature.'

What's he up to now, thought Barry, *is he going to tell me he's in trouble with his bookie and wants a loan from the imprest account.* 'Sir, a confidence, is a confidence, whether it be official, or private and you can trust me to keep it to myself.'

Tremayne smiled. 'Splendid, Barry, I knew I could rely on you. In spite of the minor differences of opinion that have occurred from time-to-time, which have necessitated me taking a strong line with you and the crew, we've all worked well as a team, and I shall not forget the loyal and efficient support you have given me when I complete your annual appraisal report and your suitability for commissioning assessment.'

Bloody hell, he's really giving me a line of soft soap. Buttering me up for something big. Better go along with it. 'Yes, sir, it really has been a great learning experience working with you and the crew, and I'm sure that the knowledge I have gained will stand me in good stead for the rest of my career in the RAF.' *That should do it. No wonder they say, "bullshit baffles brains".*

'You will, of course, be unaware of the fact, but Miss Carterton's father asked Colonel McMurchy to look out for her while she is in Bangkok. But as the colonel is up-country most of the time he asked if I would cover for him, and I agreed. This city is not the safest place in the world at the best of times, particularly for a young woman who is alone. And, we are in the middle of several countries that are at war, with Bangkok teeming with young soldiers fresh from the fighting and in need of female company. If you follow my drift, Barry.'

'I certainly do, sir.'

Tremayne produced a packet of Rothmans. 'Care for a cigarette, Barry?'

Why not, thought Barry, it'll be the first he's ever offered me, and they are only a shilling for a packet of 20! 'Yes, please.'

They lit their cigarettes and smoked in silence for a minute or two.

'Anyway, to get to the point, Barry, I have been alarmed to learn from Miss Carterton that she has been followed everywhere she has gone in the city and when she has been sitting outside the hotel in the mornings she has noticed the same shifty looking Orientals watching her every move. I'm greatly concerned about her safety and fear that there could be some sort of plot afoot to kidnap her. Her father, a self-made man in the newspaper business, is extremely wealthy, which would make her a likely victim for ruthless kidnappers. Now you may think that she, or I, should report this matter to the police, but without any positive proof, or direct harassment of Miss Carterton, by the men who seem to be shadowing her, I don't think the police would be very likely to bother about taking the matter seriously. Miss Carterton plans to leave Bangkok early next week to go to Saigon. My voluntary responsibility for her will then end. Now during the next few days I shall be very busy attending meetings at SEATO; I should have gone to one today, but wanted to have this talk with you. I should like you to keep an eye on her, particularly in the mornings. You don't have to sit with her, or accompany her anywhere, but just merge into the background and be available should she be accosted by anyone. I should also like you to take her and her luggage to the airport when she leaves Bangkok. Would you be willing to do this for me, or rather her?'

'Yes, of course, sir, but it may mean me having to do a bit of work at night to keep on top of the office work and aircraft clearances.'

'That's all right then, and I'll not be asking you to do any of my reports until she's left Bangkok. Now, it's 9.30 now, so you might as well make a start by driving down to the Oriental Hotel. You can take the Landrover and park it somewhere from which you will have vision of the rear terrace. Miss Carterton usually has her breakfast there and spends the rest of the morning on the terrace, reading and writing. When she leaves the terrace, to have luncheon in the hotel, usually at about 1 p.m., you can come straight back here.'

'What about the afternoons, doesn't she need any protection then?' Barry asked, although he had a very good idea who would be providing her *protection* in the afternoon.

'No…er…I have made arrangements with Colonel McMurchy's staff sergeant to look out for her in the afternoons, and anyway she spends most of the afternoon in her room. She says she's had enough of the sun by lunchtime and prefers to spend her afternoons in her air-conditioned room. She rarely goes out at night and if she does want to I'll make other arrangements to have someone to look out for her.'

'OK, sir, I'll switch my phone through to you and be off to the Oriental Hotel.'

'Cheerio, and take care, Barry.'

Barry threaded his way through the heavy Bangkok traffic and arrived at the Oriental Hotel at 9.50. He found a space to park from which he could view the terrace. But there was no sign of Miss Carterton. He walked over to the terrace and had a surreptitious look at the few people that were sitting there. None looked particularly shifty and still no sign of Miss Carterton. He buttonholed a young Thai waiter. *'Koon poot pah-sah ungrit bpen mai?'*

'Yes, sir, I speak very good English, what can I do for you?'

'Have you seen the *Farung* woman who has breakfast here and sits and reads for the rest of the morning?'

The waiter smacked his lips. 'Yes, sir, the lovely lady with golden hair was here this morning. She was seated there,' he said, pointing at the table nearest to the jetty.

Barry went over to the table. On it was a copy of the previous day's edition of *The Sydney Star*, which confirmed that she had been there.

Barry went back to the waiter. 'Did you see where she went? Did she go back into the hotel?'

'I don't know, sir, but I can ask at the desk for you and speak with my colleagues, who were working here earlier this morning. Her name is Miss Carterton, is it not?'

Barry nodded, 'Yes, that's her name.'

The waiter went into the hotel and returned within five minutes. 'Miss Carterton is not in her room, No. 307. One of the waitresses told me that Miss Carterton went on a river trip this morning at about 9 o'clock.'

Barry suddenly felt worried. 'A river trip—with whom?'

'Yes, sir, it is a regular feature of this hotel; boats stop at the end of the jetty and ask our patrons if they wish to have a trip up the Chao Phraya River. There are many interesting buildings and temples to see. Many tourists take advantage of the offer.'

'Yes, I'm sure that it is an interesting trip, but did the waitress see the man, or men, who crewed the boat Miss Carterton left on?'

The waiter looked perplexed. 'I can't say, sir, I think you'd better speak with this girl—her name is Srikut and she speak very good English. She went to Chulalongkorn University'

How sad, thought Barry, a university graduate and she's working as a waitress. 'Yes, please, fetch her to me.'

The waiter returned two minutes later with Srikut.

'Good morning, sir, I understand from my colleague that you seek the whereabouts of Miss Carterton, who is a guest in this hotel.'

'Yes, Srikut, that is right. I'm told that you saw her going on a river trip this morning. What is the normal duration of these trips?'

Srikut paused to think. 'They are usually no more than one hour.'

Barry looked at his watch—it was 10.20. 'You said that she left at 9 o'clock, so she should be back by now.'

Srikut nodded.

'Now, this is very important, can you tell me anything about the boat or its crew?'

'Yes, sir, the boat was a very expensive looking cabin cruiser. It was much bigger than the usual boats that ply for hire. Unlike most other riverboats, it had the Thai flag flying from the stern. So it was probably used outside Thai waters. There were three men on the boat. They were all dressed in expensive city clothes and did not look like the roughly clothed river men who make the river trips. One man approached Miss Carterton and seemed to be inviting her to take a cruise with them. They spoke together for a minute or two and then Miss Carterton boarded the boat and it shot off down the river at great speed.'

Thank heavens I found someone with a bit of sense, thought Barry, as he gave Srikut two five baht notes, one for her and one for her colleague.

Barry thought: *Now, should I report straight back to the group captain, or tell the police that I suspect that she has been abducted. No, I'd better wait for at least another half hour. Perhaps the boat has gone out to sea and around the coast a bit. I'll wait until one o'clock when she normally goes inside for lunch. She will have told the boat men when she wanted to return for lunch and would want sufficient time when she came back to have a shower and change her clothes after a sweltering hot morning on the river.*

Barry bought a large bottle of ice-cold lemonade and sat in the Landrover, smoking and drinking, and waited until one o'clock, but still no sign of Miss Carterton. Time to go and report her absence to the group captain. Barry was just about to pull away from his parking spot when he noticed the group captain's official car pulling in to a parking bay at the side of the hotel. Odd, very odd and why wasn't Samarn driving him? Barry got out of the Landrover and went to the car, arriving as Tremayne was getting out. Tremayne was dressed in casual civvies. So he wasn't attending a military meeting.

'Good afternoon, sir, I'm glad you're here. I've some—'

'What are you doing here, Barry?' snapped Tremayne. 'I told you to return to the embassy as soon as Miss Carterton went in for luncheon.'

'That's what I was trying to explain. Miss Carterton is not here! I was just about to leave for the embassy when you arrived. Apparently Miss Carterton went on a river cruise at nine o'clock this morning and hasn't returned.'

'How do you know about her going on a cruise?'

'I questioned the waiters. One saw her leave. Look, her newspaper is still on the table where she sat this morning.'

Tremayne looked worried. 'Tell me everything you found out from the waiters.' Tremayne listened intently while Barry gave him a full account of what he had learned from the waiters.

'I thought it would be better to let you know about what had happened before I reported the matter to the police. But as you hadn't told me what meeting you were attending this afternoon I was in a bit of a quandary.'

'Police! No, we don't want to involve them. There's probably a simple explanation as to why she hasn't returned to the hotel. She may have seen something of interest to her on the trip and got off the boat and gone to explore, perhaps even to interview the local people for a feature in her father's newspaper. As to the meeting, it was cancelled at the last minute, so I thought I'd take the opportunity, which might have been my last, to say farewell to Miss Carterton before she left for Saigon.'

Barry, listened, disbelievingly, at the unconcerned way in which the group captain was telling what to most would sound like a plausible explanation. But Barry knew differently. Something very sinister had happened to Miss Carterton and Tremayne probably had a very good idea what it was, but was choosing to keep it close to his chest. And the cancellation of the meeting and his excuse for coming to the hotel was complete fiction. Miss Carterton wasn't going for at least four days, so Tremayne would have, quite naturally, called to see her much nearer the time she was to leave. No, the randy old sod had a secret assignation with her. He'd probably been coming here every afternoon, when he had said he was attending meetings that had never been recorded in the office appointments' diary.

'Barry, you'd better get back to the embassy, just in case Miss Carterton should call there. I'll have a word with the hotel manager and leave a note for Miss Carterton. Then I'll hang around for an hour or so and see you at the embassy later. Oh, and Barry, not a word about this to anyone. I wouldn't want a garbled account of this affair to reach her father and cause him unnecessary worry.'

'Very well, sir,' said Barry, as he started to walk to the Landrover.

❦   ❦   ❦

Barry was back in the embassy catching up with the latest batch of requests from Singapore for RAF aircraft overflights of Thailand.

'Your boss missed a good meeting at SEATO this morning,' said Diana, trying to draw Barry into having a conversation since Roy Hughes, her normal target for the exchange of office gossip, was down at the docks with the naval attaché.

'Hmm,' murmured, Barry, without looking up from the signal he was reading.

But Diana wasn't to be put off. 'Yes, it was very interesting. It was all about drugs. The General Secretary said that the Laotian drug lords were processing masses of drugs from the poppies grown in Burma and the Golden Triangle. Drugs such as opium, and freebase cocaine and heroin and these drugs are being smuggled into Thailand and Vietnam. The Pathet Lao Communists buy, or steal drugs from the drugs lords and smuggle them to the drug dealers in South Vietnam. The North Vietnamese Army and the Viet Cong encourage this in the hope that these drugs will find their way into the American and other SEATO forces' bases and be taken into use by the troops. Imagine the situation, the SEATO troops all high on drugs. It could be disastrous for the—'

'Yes, all very interesting,' interrupted Barry, 'but I must get on with my work. The group captain is coming in later this afternoon and he's bound to have lots of bits and pieces for me to sort out.'

'Oh, so the group captain is going to grace us with his presence this afternoon,' Diana said maliciously. 'It's becoming rare for him to be here in the afternoon. I wonder what he gets up to every afternoon? Has he got a bit on the side while Mrs Tremayne is in the UK?'

'No, he just happens to attend a lot of secret meetings with Thai and American officers,' replied Barry, trying to end the conversation. 'He doesn't even tell me when they are to occur.'

'Anyway, Colonel Purvis thought the meeting was very informative and he thinks the group captain should be made aware of what went on before the minutes are circulated. He asked me to type up the notes I made at the meeting and let your boss have a copy.'

'Oh, great, I'm sure the group captain will be most appreciative. Now please—'

'Appreciative of what?' Asked Tremayne as he entered the general office.

'Diana is typing you some notes about what went on at the SEATO meeting this morning—'

The ringing telephone ended Barry's conversation. 'Yes, this is Group Captain Tremayne's office; who's calling, please? Mr Woo, just a moment please,' said Barry. He turned to Tremayne. 'Shall I switch it through to your office, sir?'

For a moment Tremayne looked uncertain. 'Yes, do that,' he said and went into his office and shut the door.

'What do you want, Woo? We've got nothing to talk about now that I've got my IOUs back.'

Woo laughed, 'On the contrary, we have much to talk about. But first, is your phone secure?'

'Yes, of course it is,' snapped Tremayne. 'Now get on with what you've got to tell me, or get off the line!'

'We have your Miss Ruby Carterton.'

'What! Why have you involved her in my gambling affairs?'

'It is nothing to do with your gambling affairs that we hold her. She is merely a pawn, or perhaps I should say, a queen, in our great game. We wish to induce you to perform a service for us. I have already given you the details. It is simply for you to make a return flight to Vientiane and bring some cargo to Bangkok for us. When you have done that we shall release Miss Carterton.'

'Damn you Woo, you don't think for one moment that you can get away with this. It's kidnapping and the police will be after you before you can say Jack Robinson!'

'Come now, Tremayne, you are just whistling in the dark. You know very well that you can't seek assistance from the police, or Jack Robinson, whoever he is. If you did you might find yourself having to explain your murder of three of my employees.'

'Three? I killed only two, in self-defence! It was your hot headed Laotian gunslinger who killed your Korean.'

'If it were self-defence in the case of my man Ming, why did you not report the matter to the police instead of throwing him into the klong that runs alongside your garden? I knew that Ming's body had to be somewhere on your property. You couldn't have taken it anywhere else on your own, and it couldn't have been kept in the house, because it would have soon made an unpleasant smell that would have made it easy to locate. And as there were no signs of fresh digging in your garden, it had to be that you had put him in the klong. My men found him there when they were secretly searching your house and garden. I told them to leave him there. So, you see, Tremayne, you now work for me, that is, unless you want Miss Carterton to end up dead in your klong with Ming.'

'OK, all right, let me know exactly what you want me to do and I'll do it, but I shall want some sort of guarantee that no harm comes to Miss Carterton.'

'Nothing unpleasant will happen to Miss Carterton if you follow my instructions. I shall telephone you at your home when I am ready to give you details of what is required of you. In the meantime, your silence will ensure Miss Carterton's survival.'

CHAPTER 28

❀

'Good morning, sir,' said Barry, as Tremayne passed him in the front corridor of the embassy to enter his office. 'I'm afraid I've got some bad news for you.'

Tremayne blanched. 'Bad news—it's not concerning Miss Carterton, is it?'

'No, it's Harry Simmons; he's been admitted to hospital. He became very unwell last night and we had to call in Doctor Herschmeir. He examined Harry and his initial diagnosis was that Harry had a severe case of angina and was likely to suffer a heart attack if he wasn't admitted to hospital for intensive care. He arranged for an ambulance to take him to hospital immediately.'

'Oh, that's too bad. But I've noticed just lately that Harry has not been too bright and his reactions have been very slow when he has been up front with me in the Devon. Hospital is probably the best place for him. Check his condition with the hospital daily and keep me informed of his progress.'

Not much sympathy there, thought Barry. 'Yes, Joe and I can take it in turn to visit Harry daily. Just one thing, sir, what about a replacement navigator? Do you want me to signal HQ FEAF to send one up from Singapore?'

Tremayne thought, *if I haven't got a navigator I could tell Woo that I am unable to make this mysterious flight to Vientiane. If I do that there is no need for him to hold Ruby.* 'No, Barry, hang fire on that one for a bit. I'll let you know when I want a replacement navigator up here.' Tremayne walked to his office door and then turned to Barry. 'I've got some urgent reports to draft, so please ensure that I'm not disturbed this afternoon.'

'Very well, sir,' said Barry.

Tremayne entered his office, sat down at his desk, took the hip flask out of his briefcase and took a generous swig of Remy Martin. He then lit a Rothman and drew smoke down deep into his lungs until he coughed dryly. That's better, he thought. Now to settle Woo's hash. He dialled the Lucky Strike Casino.

'Hello, who calls, please?' a woman asked.

'Group Captain Tremayne. I want to speak to Mr Woo—is he there?'

'Yes, sir, wait a moment please and I will call him to the phone.'

Woo's angry voice came on the line. 'Tremayne, the arrangement I made was that I would telephone *you* when I wanted you to make the flight to Vientiane. I—'

'You can *forget* your arrangement,' Tremayne interrupted. 'I can't fly to Vientiane, or to anywhere else for you. My navigator has been admitted to hospital and is likely to be there for a long time. And even when he is released he will have to go down to Singapore for a medical board which will probably find that he is unfit for further flying duties. So, that being the case, there is no point in you holding Miss Carterton. I demand that she be released immediately.'

'Tremayne, I am surprised at your attitude. You, as a gambler, should appreciate that I hold the most important trump card—Ruby Carterton. A replacement navigator can easily be obtained, but you'll not be able to replace Miss Carterton, will you? I'm quite sure that your authorities in Singapore could find another navigator to send to Bangkok.'

'Yes, but it could take several days to arrange for a replacement and I thought you wanted the job done in the next couple of days.'

'Yes, that is so. Urgency is of the utmost importance. And *that* being the case, I am going to provide you with a very experienced pilot who can also act as a navigator for your aircraft.'

Tremayne laughed. 'Don't think for one moment I'm prepared to fly to Vientiane, teamed up with some retired crop spraying Tiger Moth jockey!'

'No need for you to worry on that score. The pilot I have in mind is a very experienced military pilot, who has probably done more operational flying than you. He is also a proficient navigator and will be a most suitable flying partner for you. I shall arrange for him to contact you at your home to enable you both to get to know each other before you take to the air together.'

'What about Miss Carterton, is she all right? May I speak to her?"

'No, I'm afraid not. But I can assure you she is quite well and has suffered no harm at the hands of my men. But I have to say I find it highly amusing that you should keep referring to her as "Miss Carterton"—why not "Ruby"? After all, you have been spending most of your afternoons in bed with her. But please don't worry on that score, the knowledge of your almost open secret philandering is safe with me. As I've said before, once you have carried out the flying missions we have planned Miss Carterton, or rather "Ruby", will be returned to your bed! Goodbye, Group Captain Tremayne,' said Woo, with a laugh, as he replaced his receiver.

❦ ❦ ❦

The high-pitched ring of the front doorbell caused Tremayne to put his brandy glass down on the side table and reach for the

Nambu automatic pistol, which he had taken to keeping behind the cushion of his easy chair.

Seconds later, Sutep entered the den. Tremayne quickly slipped the pistol down between his right thigh and the side of the chair. 'Who is it, Sutep?'

'Master, an American man is at the door. He say he is Colonel Rantzen.'

Rantzen? What is he doing, calling on me at home? 'Please show him in here, Sutep.'

Tremayne quickly replaced the pistol behind the cushion. Sutep returned leading Rantzen into the den. Rantzen stood in the centre of the room, looking awkward.

'Brad, of all people, what brings you here at this time of night, and without a formal invitation? I maybe Doyen of the Attaché Corps, but I don't have an open house for colleagues to drop in without making an appointment,' said Tremayne, forcing a smile.

Rantzen moved nearer to Tremayne. 'This isn't a social call, Randy. It seems we have been thrown together in some sort of nefarious venture to ensure the release from captivity of my son and your newly acquired mistress.'

The penny dropped like a house brick.

'Brad, has a Chinaman called Han Woo recruited you to act as my navigator for a return flight to Vientiane?'

'Yeah, that's about the size of it. But for my part I'd not call it a recruitment, it was more like a *shanghaiing*!'

Tremayne put on a concerned look. 'Forgive my inhospitality, Brad. Please sit down and I'll get you a drink. Bourbon, isn't it?'

'Yes, that'll do fine,' replied Rantzen, moving another easy chair nearer to where Tremayne was sitting.

Tremayne went to the drinks table and half-filled a whisky glass with Old Crow bourbon for Rantzen and refilled his brandy glass.

'Tell me your story, Brad,' said Tremayne as he handed him his drink.

'No doubt you've heard all about my son being captured by Pathet Lao forces near Khe Sanh.' Tremayne nodded. 'Well, the man you mentioned, Woo, rang me this afternoon and told me that my son, Ben, had been handed over by the Pathet Lao to some powerful and influential Laotian drugs lord. To be held as a hostage, while I flew with you to Vientiane. He said that he held your friend, Miss Carterton, in Bangkok. It's my guess that he wants us to act as flying mules, carrying a consignment of cocaine and heroin into Bangkok for onward transmission to Saigon.'

Tremayne looked surprised. 'Drugs? How the hell, does he think he can get away with that?'

'Pretty easy, I'd say. We're both accredited diplomats, me to Bangkok and you to Bangkok, Vientiane and Phnom Penh. Your aircraft and vehicles are all carrying CD plates, so with a bit of smart organizing the drugs can be conveyed by plane via Bangkok and Phnom Penh. They can then be transported by road to the South Vietnam border, where they can be picked up by Viet Cong and taken into Saigon. From there, Viet Cong drug dealers can distribute them throughout South Vietnam, to wherever our troops, and those of our allies, are located. I'm sure you can imagine what that could do to the effectiveness of our forces. It might even affect the final outcome of the war.'

'You paint a pretty grim picture, Brad. I hadn't considered they'd want me to transport drugs. I thought, perhaps, alcohol, cigarettes, or even weapons from the Russians and Chinese, would be what they would want brought down here. But some SEATO notes our Colonel Purvis gave me this afternoon suggest that such an operation, planned and executed, as you have outlined, by a combination of drugs lords, Pathet Lao and Viet Cong forces, is not an improbable scenario. So what are your personal feelings in the matter?'

Rantzen emptied his glass and sat back in his chair. 'Randy, the way I see it is that life's a bitch and then you die. And my life's been one helluva bitch, and if I could save my son from what I know he could now be going through, I'd be willing to give my life to do it. But, you're the skipper on this trip, Randy. You have an aircraft at your personal disposal. We also have an aircraft, but Merkle would never agree to me using it for my own purposes and even if he did I couldn't justify a trip to Vientiane or Phnom Penh. So, Randy, you have to call the shots on this one.'

Tremayne refilled their glasses. 'Brad, as far as Ben is concerned, I don't think his present captors would torture him. They're not interested in the limited amount of military intelligence he has. He's simply their bargaining chip to get you to do what they want. I grant you, he'll not be enjoying his stay with them, but I don't believe he'll come to any real harm if we do as they ask.'

Rantzen suddenly looked brighter and more relaxed. 'You're probably right, Randy, I hadn't thought of it quite like that.'

'As to myself, you don't know much about my background, and even less about my life with my wife, Fiona and the relationship I have built up with Ruby Carterton. She has become the only thing I really value in life. I put her before my family, my career and, I suppose, even before my own life. So, I feel prepared to make a once only flight for Woo and his Laotian masters. But should they want us to do more I might see the matter in a different light. You probably don't know it, but what has been said about an Englishman, is that if you strike him once he will laugh, if you strike him twice he'll turn away, but if you strike him thrice, he'll kill you. What we must do is prepare ourselves for a possible double-cross. We need a backstop, weapons, and any help we can muster. Can you contribute anything of material value?'

Rantzen thought for a moment. 'I've still got my Army issue .44 Colt Double Eagle automatic and about four spare clips. That's the limit of my firepower. Of course, we hold plenty of weapons in the embassy, but they can only be generally issued on the authority of the ambassador, charge d'affaires, or defence attaché, if there is an attack upon the embassy.'

'What about manpower? Have you anyone who would support you in trying to save your son?'

Rantzen scratched his head. 'That's a tough one, Randy. It would be like asking a fellow American to be a traitor to his country. But there is one man on our staff who I have known since Korea. He was my orderly and, after a lot of string pulling, I got him accepted for aircrew training. He's now our radioman and would be a very useful guy to have in an emergency. He's also a damn good rifleman, a marksman, in fact, and is trained in the martial arts. He was so grateful to me for saving him from a service career as an officer's servant, that he once said to me: "You name it, sir, I'd go to hell and back for you. You'd only have say the word"; he'd probably ride shotgun for me. Of course, it wouldn't do for me to tell him everything about our ferrying drugs for the Communists. He hates them like poison and, I can't be sure, but I think he's the author of the saying "I'd sooner be dead than red". If I just told him that I was rescuing Ben from the Communists he'd be in there like Flynn. His name is Technical Sergeant Carl Mellors, and I'd trust him with my life.'

'Great, that's the sort of help we'll need if things go pear shaped. Just tell him that you and I have cooked up a plan to rescue your son and to keep everything under his hat.'

'That sounds OK. I'm sure he'd go along with that,' said Rantzen.

'Good. Now I've got two pistols; one of them is a small calibre Japanese Nambu automatic. I've only got 12 rounds for it and there's not much likelihood that I can get any more. The other weapon is a .38 calibre automatic, which has a silencer fitted, and would be very useful. I have two spare magazines for that gun. But take a look at these,' said Tremayne, as he rose from his chair and walked to a bookcase. Reaching behind it, he pulled out two carbines and held them out for Rantzen's inspection.

'Hells bells! Garand, .30 calibre, M1 carbines. I haven't seen one of those since Korea. You're loaded for bear! Where did you get these, Randy?'

Tremayne smiled. 'You could call them spoils of war, Brad. I've got eight 15 round magazines to go with them as well.'

'We could start a small war with what we've got,' said Brad.

'Well, I hope it doesn't have to come to that to do what we have to do,' said Tremayne as he put the carbines back behind the bookcase.

Tremayne refilled their glasses and settled back comfortably in his chair. He was beginning to get a feeling of confidence working with Rantzen. Almost looking forward to the possible action it might involve. Like Operation Market-Garden when he'd flown through a hell of flak filled sky, harassed by enemy fighters, while he dropped supplies to doomed British 1st Airborne Division, landed to take a bridge too far and surrounded by the remnants of two elite SS Panzer Divisions.

Rantzen leant forward in his chair. 'How about your crew, Randy? Would any of them help?'

'My crew! I've only got two, and one of them is in hospital. That's why I need you. My engineer is a very useful chap to have around, but I'm pretty sure that he would not involve himself in anything illegal. And my flight sergeant assistant is a pretty resourceful chap, but he is not one to stray too far from the straight and narrow, particularly if it had anything to do with drugs. Anyway, I want him to remain in Bangkok while we are away. So it looks as though it's down to you, your trusty sergeant and me, accompanied, I suppose, by one or two of Woo's gangsters to chaperone us. But now, all that we can do is to wait for Woo's signal to take off.'

'Yes, I guess you're right about that. Goodnight, Randy, I'll let myself out,' said Rantzen walking into the hall.

'Goodnight, Brad, and don't worry, we'll make a good team. We'll get your son back.'

🍁   🍁   🍁

After Brad had left, Tremayne drank the rest of the Remy Martin before taking a shower and preparing to retire for the night.

The servants had secured all the windows and shutters, but as was his normal practice, he went all around the house checking that they were closed.

He put the Nambu automatic back in the secret camera compartment of his briefcase and put the briefcase in his bureau and locked the door. He took Ming's automatic, with a silencer fitted, to his bedroom and put it under his pillows. He was just about to turn off his bedside light when the telephone rang.

He picked up the phone and quietly said, 'Hello?'

Woo's voice came over the line. 'Ah, Tremayne, I hope I haven't caught you in the shower, or just as you were about to achieve an orgasm with one of your housemaids who might be sharing your bed while your wife is in America and your mistress is enjoying my hospitality.'

Tremayne seethed. 'Yes, I'm here, on my own, and you can thank your lucky stars you're not with me. If you were you'd have my hands around your throat, slowly tightening until your eyes popped out and you made your last gasp.'

'Oh, come now, Tremayne, don't be so melodramatic. You know you wouldn't do anything that might put Ruby in jeopardy. Now control yourself and listen carefully to what I am about to say. I shan't repeat my instructions. Take notes if you feel the need. You are to proceed to Don Muang airport in your car at 0600 hours on Wednesday, the day after tomorrow. I have given Colonel Rantzen similar instructions and he should meet you there. You will be met by one of my men, who will accompany you on your flight. You, or Lieutenant Colonel Rantzen are to prepare a flight plan for a flight from Bangkok to Vientiane, thence to Phnom Penh and return to Bangkok—'

Tremayne exploded. 'What in hell's name are you playing at—'

'Be quiet, Tremayne, necessity has caused the need for a change of plan. You will take off at 0700 hours. During the flight you are to obey the instructions of my man with regard to the loading and unloading of the cargo. Please don't entertain any foolhardy notions about overcoming him and holding him as an exchange hostage for Lieutenant Rantzen or Ruby Carterton. The man is quite expendable and his loss would simply mean that the whole operation would have to be repeated. Before you land at Vientiane, you are to radio your embassy and ask them to arrange for a Landrover, or similar vehicle to be driven to the airport to meet you. Tell the embassy transport manager that you will provide your own driver to take you, alone, in the vehicle a few miles north of Vientiane. Make some excuse that you are visiting a local chieftain of the Hmong Tribes. The embassy driver can wait until the vehicle returns from its destination with the cargo. When the cargo has been off-loaded from the vehicle and loaded onto your aircraft he can return to the embassy. The same procedure is to be followed when you fly from Vientiane to Phnom Penh. The cargo will be off-loaded and put in the embassy vehicle and my man will drive you to a secret border crossing point, controlled by the Viet Cong. Viet Cong agents will transfer the cargo from your vehicle to theirs. When this has been done you will be driven back to Phnom Penh, where you will hand over the embassy vehicle to the Cambodian driver and take off for Bangkok. When you land at Don Muang you and your crew will be free to return to your respective embassies, or wherever else you wish to go. Is that clear? Have you any questions?'

'Yes, just one, when and where will you release Ruby Carterton?'

'As soon as I receive confirmation from my Laotian contacts, that the cargo has been safely received in Saigon, I shall have one of my men drive Ruby to the Oriental Hotel. I hope that satisfies your concerns about Ruby.'

The phone went dead, before Tremayne could think of a reply.

CHAPTER 29

❀

Tremayne arrived at the embassy as a chancery guard was unbolting the giant doors.

'Good morning, sir,' said the surprised guard, as Tremayne strode purposefully down the front corridor to his office.

In his office, Tremayne emptied the contents of his briefcase into a side drawer in his desk. Seeing Barry and Joe entering the building through his corridor window, he tapped on the pane and motioned them to enter his office through his corridor entrance. Both looked surprised; this had never happened before. They said, 'Good morning, sir,' in chorus, as they entered his office.

'We called into the hospital yesterday to see Harry and—'

'Never mind the medical report, Barry, just sit down and listen to what I have to tell you both. I have to fly to Vientiane early tomorrow morning. Joe, I want you to go to the airport today to make your usual pre-flight checks and see that the aircraft is fuelled to capacity and that includes the auxiliary tank in the baggage section.'

'What about a crew, sir?' asked Joe.

'I shan't need you on this trip, Joe, and I've borrowed a navigator from the US Defence Attaché.'

'Captain Mike Denver, he's an ace navigator, sir,' interposed Barry.

'I know all about Captain Denver, but it's not him I'm taking,' snapped Tremayne.

'But, sir, he's the only navigator—'

'Barry, just shut up, and listen. If you haven't any pressing duties this afternoon I want you and Joe to drive southward along the Chao Phraya River bank and see if you can spot the cabin cruiser that took Miss Carterton on her river trip. It is my strong belief that she has been kidnapped and is being held prisoner on the boat. The kidnappers will probably be trying to contact her father to negotiate a ransom payment for her release. I am very concerned about Miss Carterton's safety. She is a very attractive woman and I fear that the men holding her might take advantage of her situation to do their worst.'

'But wouldn't it be better to report your suspicions to the police?' suggested Joe.

'Absolutely not, Joe. If boatloads of uniformed Thai police, which there would be, because of her diplomatic connections and her wealthy publisher father, zipped up and down the river, their presence would almost certainly alert those who are holding her. No, I want you two to do a very covert recce. But take photographs of the boat and its crew, if you locate it. Now is that clear to you both?'

Barry was first to speak, 'Yes, perfectly clear, sir.' It was rarely advisable to question Tremayne's instructions.

'I still think it would be better to report the matter to the police and let them deal with it. And shouldn't the Australian Ambassador be doing something about it?' said Joe.

Tremayne sighed deeply. 'Yes, Joe, in normal circumstances, it would be better to leave it to the police and the victim's embassy personnel. But, I can assure you that these are *not normal* circumstances.'

Joe looked nonplussed, but mumbled, 'I understand, sir.'

Barry and Joe rose to leave the office.

'Not so fast, I haven't finished yet. I shall be landing quite late in the evening and want you both to meet me at the airport. I shall radio the embassy to let you have my ETA, Barry.'

Barry nodded.

'OK, Joe, you get down to the airport now and do what has to be done and I'll see you tomorrow. Barry, you stay and sit down, I have something more to tell you.'

Barry sat down and, like Joe had done, wondered why the group captain was so against involving the police in the search for Miss Carterton.

Tremayne placed his briefcase on the desk. He looked hard at Barry for a full minute. Barry felt uncomfortable, as if something unpleasant was about to be said, or done. But he returned Tremayne's steady gaze.

'You've been trained in the use of small arms, haven't you, Barry?'

Barry answered without wondering about the question. 'Yes, sir, Bren gun, Sten gun, .303 Lee Enfield rifle, the Belgian FN rifle, British service revolver, and the Mills 36 hand grenade.'

'Good. Do you think you could handle this weapon?' said Tremayne as he withdrew the Browning, .38 calibre automatic pistol, with silencer attached, from the secret camera pocket at the bottom of the briefcase. 'Careful, it's loaded,' he said as he handed it to Barry.

Barry took the pistol and confidently removed the sound moderator and the magazine, pushed the safety catch to the off position and pulled back the slide to eject the cartridge in the breech. He pointed the pistol at the sun streaming through Tremayne's window and looked down the barrel. 'Yes, sir, it's a fairly simple gun to operate. The magazine normally holds ten rounds, but I see there are only four in total with the one I ejected. So, presumably, it was last fired six times and hasn't been cleaned since.'

Tremayne looked at Barry admiringly. This flight sergeant is not just a shiny-arsed pen pusher. *He's certainly someone who's handled weapons, more than he would in just carrying out his annual musketry practise.* 'Where did you learn about firearms, Barry?'

'Well, as I'm sure you will be aware, sir, all airmen are given training on small arms during their basic training.'

'Yes, I know that, but it must have been nearly 20 years ago when you did your basic training.'

'Yes, it was. But I should have mentioned the fact that I did a tour of duty, as the squadron orderly room clerk, with an RAF Regiment squadron in Germany and the squadron commander insisted that all the support personnel, clerks, storemen, cooks, armourers, vehicle fitters, etc., had to go out on manoeuvres and fire on the various ranges with the rifle and mortar flight men. The high spot of the tour, I suppose, was the squadron's deployment in Berlin. We were barracked with the Welsh Guards at Gatow, a very short distance from the Russian Zone that surrounded Berlin. We played cat and mouse with the Ruskies by placing empty radio caravans on a field between their lines and ours. This caused them much consternation and they were forever flying over to take aerial photographs of our "secret weapons". If nothing else it used up a lot of Russian aircraft fuel and film. I quite enjoyed this experience, and sometimes wished I hadn't been mustered into the RAF as an administrator. I think I'd have been better employed in the RAF Regiment, or even in the Army.'

'Yes, I believe you could be right there, Barry. But tell me, have you ever shot and killed anyone, or even fired your weapon in anger?'

What is this leading to? thought Barry. *He's not giving me this grilling for something to talk about.* 'Well, I certainly hope I've never killed anybody. But one night in Egypt, when I was the corporal in charge of a section, guarding a fleet of Wimpey's lorries that were stuck in the sand near Tel El Kebir, I did loose off a magazine load of bullets at a gang of cliftie wallahs, who failed to answer my challenge; you know the sort of thing: "Halt, who goes there?…Halt, or I fire." They didn't halt, so I fired ten times, aiming, as I thought, just above their heads. We searched the area in the morning for any casualties, but found no bodies, so I suppose they were all lucky short-arses.'

Tremayne should have laughed at the punch line to the story—most people did—but he didn't. 'Have you considered, Barry, that the dead and wounded could have been carried away by their fellow thieves or, more likely, buried in the sand where they fell?'

Barry didn't like the way the conversation was turning. It seemed as though Tremayne was deliberately trying to get him to accept that he could be ruthless if put under pressure. Barry tried to make light of it by forcing a laugh. 'I never thought about it like that, but was pleased when the night ended. It was pretty scary. But the contractors did thank us for guarding their vehicles, which, but for our presence, would have disappeared, piece-by-piece, during the night.'

Tremayne smiled. 'Sounds like you should have received an RAF "Good Show" award for what you did.'

Barry rose to leave the office. 'Will that be all for now, sir?'

'No, not quite, I want you to take this briefcase and keep the pistol in the bottom compartment. There are also two spare ammo clips with it. Keep the briefcase with you at all times, but don't mention anything about the gun to Joe.'

'But, sir, shouldn't I be in possession of a Thai firearms permit to own, or carry this weapon?'

'Yes, technically, you should, but don't worry yourself about that. In the unlikely event that the police should find out about it,

I can deal with the matter through diplomatic channels. Having said that, I wouldn't want you to think for one moment that I expect you to have to use the weapon. You should consider its use as a last resort, if you should find yourself, or Miss Carterton, in a dangerous confrontation with the men who are holding her. It is my firm belief that they are most likely to be professional criminals and extremely dangerous. One last point, search diligently for that cabin cruiser, but take no direct action unless it is unavoidable. I'll expect to find you waiting at the airport when I return tomorrow evening. Take care, Barry.'

Barry picked up the briefcase from Tremayne's desk and took it to the office strong room and locked it in the air attaché's safe.

CHAPTER 30

Lieutenant Colonel Brad Rantzen and Technical Sergeant Carl Mellors were drinking coffee in the departure lounge when Tremayne parked his official car in the parking bay at the rear of the lounge. He joined Rantzen and Mellors. Rantzen introduced Mellors to Tremayne, who was immediately impressed by Mellors' firm handshake, upright stance, and his ruggedly handsome, but tough looking, heavy-featured face. A no-nonsense NCO, he thought.

'From where do you hail, sergeant?' questioned Tremayne for something to say.

'Pittsburgh, Pennsylvania, sir.'

'Yes, I know all about Pittsburgh,' said Tremayne with a wry smile. 'Tell me, is that pawnshop still on the corner?'

They all laughed at Tremayne's weak joke, but Tremayne felt that a bond had been made with his two companions and he felt better than he had done for days.

While they sat talking and drinking coffee an oriental man approached their table. A Woo man, no doubt about it, thought Tremayne.

Addressing Tremayne, he asked, 'You are Group Captain Tremayne, are you not?'

Tremayne nodded.

'Mr Woo, my employer, told me that I was to fly with you to Vientiane and Phnom Penh this morning.'

'Yes, you are to be my passenger,' replied Tremayne. Then to Rantzen and Mellors: 'If you've done the business with air traffic control, Brad, and finished your coffee chaps, let's saddle up and get airborne.'

'Yes, everything's ready to go, Randy,' confirmed Rantzen as they left the departure lounge.

The four men climbed into the Devon. Tremayne and Rantzen went forward to the flight deck and Mellors and Feng sat apart in two of the passenger seats, eyeing each other with suspicion.

'Where do you want to refuel?' asked Rantzen. 'We've got over 1800 kilometres flying in front of us and this aircraft's range is just a little more than 1400 kilometres.'

Tremayne looked thoughtful. 'Refuelling, that's something I rarely have to think about. I usually leave that sort of thing to my engineer. He sees that I never run out of fuel. I suppose, we'd better top up at Vientiane for the long haul down to Phnom Penh. That should then see us right to get back to Don Muang.'

'When I was doing the flight plan, I had to do some calculations as to our ETAs and ETDs here, at Vientiane, Phnom Penh and back here. The aircraft has a maximum cruising speed of 210 mph. I averaged our flight times based on 200 mph, which means that we shall be in the air for about six hours and, in order for the collection and delivery of the cargo to be made, the same time on the ground. Which means, of course, that we shan't be back here until 1900 hours this evening.'

Tremayne grinned widely. 'That's exactly what I figured, Brad. Now that's enough gassing, let's get up into the wide blue yonder.'

Two minutes later, exactly as planned, the Devon was airborne, flying in a northeasterly direction.

The flight was uneventful. Mellors kept the two officers supplied with cold water and fruit juices, while he drank most of the stock of San Miguel beer. Feng sat reading a book and never spoke a word to Mellors. When he did look up at Mellors, it was with a sullen look on his face, which did not invite conversation.

About half an hour before they were due to land at Vientiane, Tremayne radioed the British Embassy and asked that the transport manager arrange to have someone meet them at the airport with a long-based Landrover.

Tremayne made a near perfect landing and taxied the aircraft to the pre-arranged parking space. The Landrover was parked nearby and its Laotian driver was leaning against the bonnet smoking.

Feng suddenly became alive, issuing orders. He ordered the driver to hand over the vehicle keys and gave him a handful of Laotian Kip notes and told him to go and get a meal and wait for their return. 'Group Captain Tremayne, you are to come with me in the Landrover. But before you get into the vehicle I must search you for hidden weapons. Mr Woo warned me that you might have a gun or knife hidden about your person. Raise your arms please.' Feng ran his hands expertly over Tremayne's lightly clad body. 'Good, no weapons, you may enter the vehicle. And you,' Feng said, turning to Rantzen 'and your sergeant are to stay with the aircraft until we return.'

Tremayne climbed into the front passenger seat of the Landrover and Feng drove off at great speed heading northwards, on a road that was unfamiliar to Tremayne. Feng never spoke, or took his eyes off the road ahead. Tremayne sat chain smoking, looking out of the window as the vehicle passed out of the city and into the wild and largely uncultivated countryside.

After about an hour they approached a large wooden building with several adjacent outbuildings, surrounded by an eight-foot high, heavy chain-link fence. Several men were patrolling inside the fence. Some held straining Dobermans on chain leads and others carried automatic weapons. As Feng drove up to the gate of the complex, two men ran to the gate and, recognising Feng, opened it. Feng drove the Landrover to the bottom of the wooden stairs that lead to the main entrance of the building. Feng got out of the Landrover and spoke in Lao to the gate men, who disappeared into one of the outbuildings. Feng motioned Tremayne to join him at the steps of the building. As they stood there the main entrance door opened and a man appeared and beckoned them to ascend the stairs and enter the building. The man, who looked to be a Eurasian, was of indeterminate age. He was dressed in a white linen suit. He was well over six feet tall and slimly built. His sallow skinned features were Caucasian, but his almond shaped eyes betrayed his Asian origin. His head was completely hairless. He raised his arms as if to greet a long time friend. 'Welcome, Group Captain Tremayne. We haven't met before, so I should introduce myself. My name is George Lloyd. Odd, you might think, that a Eurasian, as I am, should bear such a name. It was my Welsh father's choice. Much against my Laotian mother's wishes, but my father's sense of humour prevailed. But now to business. I am so pleased that you have decided to enter my service. You will be appropriately rewarded for what you are doing.'

Tremayne didn't reply but shrugged his shoulders resignedly, as a Frenchman would.

Lloyd clapped his arm around Feng's shoulders and said something to him in Lao, which seemed to please Feng. His face was wreathed in smiles as he left them to join the men who were now loading large sacking covered bales of cocaine and heroin into the Landrover.

'Please now join me for some refreshment in my home, group captain. I understand from Woo that you are, as I am, appreciative of fine cognacs. I have the very best.'

Lloyd led Tremayne into a large room, furnished in luxurious Asian style furniture and tapestries. A small bar was built into one corner of the room and perched on a barstool was one of the most beautiful oriental women Tremayne had ever seen. She was sipping a cocktail and smoking a cigarette in a long jade holder. Lloyd clapped his hands and she immediately placed her drink on the bar, stubbed out her cigarette and jumped off the barstool. Lloyd spoke to her in Lao and she half filled two brandy balloons with cognac. Lloyd handed one to Tremayne.

'What is it that is said in your country when two friends have drink together—cheers, I believe,' said Lloyd with a high-pitched laugh.

'That's about right Mr Lloyd. That is what is sometimes said when *friends* drink together. But you are being very presumptuous in thinking of me as your friend. I'm performing this service, as you put it, in return for the release of two people from your captivity. Namely Ruby Carterton, held by your slimy henchman, Woo, somewhere in Bangkok, and Lieutenant Ben Rantzen, who, I understand, is probably held by you here.'

'Oh, what a pity you don't see the value of a partnership with me. I could make you a wealthy man. I need a reliable and able pilot, particularly one who has the freedom of movement that you have.'

'You'll have to think again on that score. As much as I like money and badly need it, I'd not involve myself in carrying illegal drugs for a living.'

'Oh, but you already have. I arranged for Feng to secret a quantity of heroin on your aircraft before you left Bangkok. Possession of heroin or other hard drugs with intention to sell them in Thailand is punishable by death. But I've no wish to depress you, Group Captain Tremayne. Please let me refill your glass.' Lloyd snapped his fingers and the Asian beauty refilled both their glasses.

Tremayne looked out of the window and saw that Lloyd's men had finished loading the Landrover and were standing about the vehicle, smoking and talking to Feng.

Tremayne turned to Lloyd. 'There's one thing I want from you before I leave with those drugs, and that is to have a look at Lieutenant Ben Rantzen.'

Lloyd made an expansive gesture with his hands. 'Why certainly, Group Captain, you may see him, to assure yourself that he is being well looked after. Please follow me.' Lloyd led Tremayne down a passage to the rear of the building. He stopped at the door where a man sat with a sub-machine gun across his knees. The man immediately got to his feet and opened the door to the room. Tremayne followed Lloyd into the room and saw that its only window had steel bars screwed to its frame.

Lieutenant Rantzen was sitting in an easy chair. His feet were shackled together and his left arm was handcuffed to the arm of the chair. A large jug of water and a glass were on a side table within reach of his right hand. Two Laotians were seated, across from Ben, at a small table playing cards. Both carried shoulder holstered automatic pistols.

Tremayne went to Ben Rantzen, who looked up at Tremayne with a look of relief in his eyes.

'I'm Group Captain Randolph Tremayne, a colleague and friend of your father's, and I'm trying to secure your release.'

'I'm sure pleased to see you, sir. My father has spoken about you. You are the Doyen of the Military Attaché Corps, aren't you?'

Tremayne nodded. 'Yes, but never mind that now. How are they treating you? I see you are clean and shaven. Are you getting enough to eat?'

'I'm being treated a lot better than when I was first captured by the Pathet Lao. They roughed me up a bit when they were questioning me. But it didn't last long after they found out that I knew less than they did about our deployments in their area of operations. How soon am I going to be—'

'That's enough,' interrupted Lloyd. 'You've seen and heard enough to know that this young officer has not been ill-treated while he has been in our custody, and it's time, Tremayne, for you to be on your way to Phnom Penh.'

Tremayne shook Ben's hand. 'Goodbye for now, Ben, and hang in there—we'll have you out of here as soon as we can.'

'Goodbye, sir, and thanks for what you are doing and please give my love to my Father.'

'I will, I promise I will, Ben,' said Tremayne as he followed Lloyd back into the passage and out of the building.

Outside, Lloyd called to Feng. 'Off you go now and telephone me at every stop until you reach the South Vietnam border crossing.'

'Yes, Mr Lloyd, I will do as you command. Come, Tremayne, get back in the vehicle.'

The journey back to Vientiane airport was uneventful. Tremayne spent the time smoking and looking out of the window and thinking about how he, Rantzen and Mellors, might bring about the release of Ben against Lloyd's force of well-armed henchmen.

Arriving at the airport, Feng drove the Landrover alongside the Devon and then ordered Rantzen and Mellors, who were sitting inside the aircraft, to start unloading the Landrover and transferring the bales of drugs to the Devon. As soon as they had been loaded, Tremayne and Rantzen climbed into their seats and Mellors and Feng returned to their passenger seats.

Tremayne checked the fuel gauge. 'I see you've had her fuelled to capacity, Brad.'

'Yeah, skipper, it's all systems go.'

'Brad, you'll be happy to know, I saw Ben and he seems OK. I promised him we'd get him out. He asked me to convey his love to you.'

'Thanks, Randy, I'll not forget that. For a Limey, you're a pretty stand-up guy.'

Tremayne smiled as he opened the throttle and fired the engines. Moments later the Devon roared down the runway and soared into the air, en route for Phnom Penh.

Thirty minutes from touch down, Tremayne radioed the British Embassy in Phnom Penh and requested that a Landrover or small truck be delivered at the airport for his use. 'I want to check first hand on what's happening along the Cambodian border with South Vietnam,' he lied to the embassy transport manager.

On landing at Phnom Penh the vehicle was waiting, with the driver in his seat, smoking. Feng gave him a fistful of Cambodian Riel notes and told him to go and find somewhere to have a meal and to wait for his return. When the driver was out of sight, Feng ordered the drugs to be off-loaded from the aircraft and transferred to the Landrover. As soon as the drugs had been loaded he jumped into the driver's seat. Tremayne got in beside him.

Tremayne, conscious of the fact that he was beginning to tire and that he would feel even worse after the drive to the South Vietnam border and back to Phnom Penh, for a flight back to Bangkok, he went to sleep. He had no fear of Feng harming him while they were on the road. He was needed to show his diplomatic credentials, which included his photograph, to any police or other officials who might stop them on the road.

Feng, roughly shaking his shoulder, awakened Tremayne. 'We are at the border. Have your documents ready in case we are challenged by Cambodian border patrols.'

Tremayne sat up straight in his seat and withdrew his wallet in readiness.

Feng drove under some overhanging trees and switched off the vehicle lights.

Tremayne guessed that Feng had stopped at a pre-arranged point on the border. He was proved right by the almost immediate arrival of six heavily armed men. Feng got out of the Landrover and approached the men and quietly exchanged greetings with them. Four of the men placed their weapons on the ground and came over to the Landrover. Feng opened the rear doors and the men quickly, but quietly, unloaded the bales and carried them through the trees and undergrowth to their vehicle, which was out of sight of the Landrover. Their task completed, the four men recovered their weapons and returned to their vehicle. The two remaining Viet Cong agents talked with Feng for a few minutes. One handed him a large hessian bag and they then disappeared through the trees. A minute later Tremayne heard the sound of the Viet Cong agents' vehicle driving away. Feng, with a smug look on his ugly face, climbed into his seat and put the hessian bag on the floor behind his legs. Feng, the smug look still on his face, turned to Tremayne. 'We now return to Phnom Penh,' he said, as he released the vehicle's handbrake and quietly drove away from the rendezvous.

Tremayne, refreshed by his nap, decided to stay awake during the journey back to Phnom Penh. He badly wanted a drink, but he had left his hip flask on the Devon, so he occupied himself by looking out of the window and smoking while he thought about what was to happen next. Now that he had successfully completed Lloyd's mission, presumably Lloyd would communicate with Woo and tell him to release Ruby. Ben Rantzen's release and return to Saigon, via Bangkok, was another matter. Lloyd might just turn him loose across the Laotian border to South Vietnam, or put him on an aircraft from Vientiane to Bangkok or Saigon. That was a matter to discuss with Brad Rantzen when he got back to Phnom Penh.

CHAPTER 31

After Joe had returned from the airport the previous day, he and Barry had driven along the roads bordering the Chao Phraya River, searching for the cabin cruiser, crewed by the possible abductors of Miss Carterton. They were out again, from first light, driving further down towards the river estuary. Joe was at the wheel, driving as slow as traffic conditions would permit, and Barry was scanning both sides of the river with binoculars, for any sign of a cabin cruiser with a Thai flag on the stern. They passed several vessels displaying the Thai national flag, but none that resembled the description Barry had obtained from the Oriental Hotel waitress.

Joe suddenly stopped the vehicle. 'It's time for a break, Barry, I'm gasping a drink.'

'OK, Joe, but it'll have to be water this time. There's no beer left. You drank it all yesterday.'

Barry pulled two bottles of water from their cool box and handed one to Joe. They both drank and Barry passed a cigarette to Joe and lit one for himself.

'We'll stay here for 15 minutes and then push on, but keep your eyes peeled on this nearside bank and I'll scan the opposite bank with the binoculars,' said Barry.

Joe glanced out of the window on Barry's side and almost jumped out of his seat with excitement. 'There it is, Barry, look, under that clump of trees overhanging the river. It's got a flag hanging from the stern.'

Barry looked out and scanned the clump of trees with the binoculars. 'You're right; it's the boat we're looking for. I can see its name on the stern. It's called *The Lucky Strike*.'

'*The Lucky Strike*,' repeated Joe. 'That's a coincidence; there's a nightclub called *The Lucky Strike*. I've heard Tremayne telling Samarn to drive him there.'

Barry continued scanning the boat for signs of life aboard. A few minutes passed and a man dressed in a dark suit appeared on deck, leaned on the rail and lit a cigarette. *He's dressed as the waitress had described—it must be the boat we want*, thought, Barry. *Now to find out who owns the boat.* 'Joe, do you know where the Harbour Master's office is?'

'Sure, I've driven the naval attaché and Hughes there several times; it's back up river a mile or two.'

'Good, so that's where we are going to find out who owns that craft,' said Barry, a plan beginning to formulate in his mind.

A few minutes later Joe stopped the Landrover in front of the Harbour Master's office.

'You stay with the vehicle, Joe, and I'll have a word with someone inside.'

Barry got out of the vehicle and went to the office. He went to the office marked "Enquiries" in English and Thai, and rang the bell. A smartly dressed young man came to the enquiry office counter. 'How may I help you, sir?' he enquired in perfect English.

'*Sawadee Krup*,' replied Barry, thinking it was just as well to be polite to the man. It might ensure his help in eliciting the information he wanted. 'I am trying to trace the owner of the cabin cruiser named *The Lucky Strike*.'

The young man beamed. 'That is an easy question. The boat is owned by Mr Han Woo.'

Barry could hardly contain his excitement. 'Does Mr Woo also own a nightclub called *The Lucky Strike*?'

'Yes, sir, he does. He also owns much other property in Bangkok. As you English would say: he has a finger in many pies,' said the young man with a laugh.

'*Korp koon, krup*,' said Barry with a smile. 'You have been very helpful.'

Barry quickly got back into the Landrover. 'We've got him, Joe. It's a man called Han Woo who owns the boat and he owns and lives at his nightclub—*The Lucky Strike*.'

'What do we do now then—go to the police?'

'No, Joe, not the police, remember what the group captain said about them getting involved? I have a plan. Let's get back to the house and I'll explain all.'

Back at their house, Barry and Joe showered and changed their clothes. When Barry came back from his room, Joe was opening beer cans. 'Here's one for you, Barry.'

'Thanks, Joe, but we'll have to make this just one. We need clear heads to carry off what I've got planned.'

'Well, let's hear what you've got in mind,' said Joe, making himself comfortable in a large cane armchair.

Barry sat down and didn't stop talking for several minutes. 'What do you think about that then, Joe?'

'It all sounds a bit James Bondish, but it could be a good way to spend an otherwise boring afternoon,' answered Joe.

'Right then, let's get what we need and get on down to the river,' said Barry, emptying his glass.

Arriving at the point on the riverbank opposite to where they had seen *The Lucky Strike*, Barry looked across the river at the clump of trees. The boat was still there. He and Joe walked along the bank until they located a small jetty and saw two or three small motorboats tied to a rail. They located the owner of one of the boats and negotiated the hire of the boat.

'My friend here will drive the boat. He is an engineer and knows everything there is to know about engines. We shall need the boat for about one hour and return it to you.'

The Thai boat owner was not very happy that they didn't want him to drive the boat. 'It is not that I don't trust you, but it is the insurance.'

'How much is it to hire your boat for one hour if you are driving it?' asked Barry.

'For one hour I charge 30 baht,' said the boatman.

'Then, if you let us take it out for one hour on our own, I shall give you 100 baht,' said Barry, holding out a 100 baht note.

The man snatched the note from Barry. 'For 100 baht you may hire my boat, and go where you please, but bring it back in one hour—undamaged.'

The boatman untied the rope that secured the boat and waved them off. Barry with his briefcase, and Joe with a hessian bag, climbed into the boat and Joe fired the engine.

'Take her past the Woo's boat and cross over to the other side of the river and bring her up close behind those overhanging trees and out of sight of this side of the river,' said Barry.

Joe slowly drove the motorboat to the stern of *The Lucky Strike*, and cut the engine.

'Ahoy, aboard!' shouted Barry.

A few seconds passed and two men came to the stern rail. 'What do you want?' said the older of the two men.

'Are you Han Woo?' asked Barry.

The man nodded.

'Well, I'm Perry Brown; a private enquiry agent employed by Murray Carterton, the father of Miss Ruby Carterton. Mr Carterton believes his daughter is being held by you on this vessel against her will.'

Woo laughed loudly. 'What an outrageous suggestion! Whatever gave Carterton such a ridiculous idea?'

'It's no joke, Woo. Carterton has had detectives of my agency watching your boat for over two days and two of your men were seen by the Oriental Hotel staff taking Miss Carterton down river in this boat.'

'OK, Brown, supposing it were true and I did have Miss Carterton aboard, what would Carterton, or you, do about it?'

'Well, if we had a mind to, we could go to the police. But Carterton does not want to involve the Thai police or the Australian Embassy, but would rather negotiate with you for the release of his daughter. He is a very wealthy man and is prepared to offer you 50,000 US dollars for the immediate release of his daughter.'

Woo gasped. Could this possibly be true? If it were, he could finish with Lloyd, sell the casino, and retire to somewhere like Bali, or Hawaii. 'Have you the money with you, Mr Brown?'

'Yes, I have it in this briefcase. Five-hundred, used, 100-dollar bills and it's all yours when you bring Miss Carterton up on the deck and release her to my care.'

'Very well, Mr Brown, tell your boatman to bring this boat around to the side of mine and I'll have a ladder lowered for you to come aboard.'

'That's OK, Woo, but while I'm climbing aboard I want to see Miss Carterton standing on the deck.'

'As soon as you have sight of her, I shall want to see the money,' replied Woo.

'Bring the boat around to the side,' whispered Barry to Joe.

Woo's man hung a metal ladder over the side of the motor cruiser.

Barry climbed slowly up the steps. As he reached the top and was about to climb over the rail, Woo shouted an instruction in Lao to his henchman, whose hand went under his jacket and reappeared in a flash with an automatic pistol held in it and pointed at Barry.

'Watch him, Wong, while I fetch Miss Carterton for his inspection,' said Woo to his gunman.

A minute later Woo reappeared, with another man, who was leading Ruby. Her hands were tied behind her back.

'Here she is, Mr Brown. Now let me see the money.'

Barry opened the brief case and reached inside.

'Stay your hand, Brown; I've seen that briefcase before. The gold initials "R.T." stand for Randolph Tremayne. If anything but a packet of 100-dollar bills is in your hand when it comes out of the briefcase, Wong will shoot you dead!'

Barry knew that if he drew the gun from the briefcase Wong would kill him. He had to have an edge to beat the gunman. There was only one thing he could do. He lifted the briefcase chest high, as if to show Woo its contents and shouted, 'Let them go, Joe,' as he squeezed the trigger of the Browning automatic and fired twice through the leather briefcase. The force of the bullets hitting his chest threw Wong back and, as he fell dead, his finger involuntarily squeezed the trigger of his pistol, firing a bullet upwards, which hit Woo in the back of his head and lifted a chunk off his skull. As Woo fell to the deck two Molotov cocktails sailed over the rail, hit the boat's cabin roof, exploded and sprayed burning petrol over the wheelhouse, the deck and the remaining gunman, who ran, his trousers ablaze, screaming to the side of the vessel and reached for his shoulder-holstered weapon. Barry removed his pistol from the briefcase, took deliberate aim at the gunman's chest and fired once. The gunman, his clothing now ablaze, dropped his pistol and fell dead on the burning deck.

Barry dropped the briefcase and quickly untied Ruby's wrists. 'Ruby, down the ladder and into the speedboat, as quick as you can.' Ruby needed no second bidding, as the burning petrol swept across the deck to where they were standing.

With Ruby safely aboard the speedboat and Joe at the wheel, and ready for the off, Barry started to descend the ladder. In a flash he thought: *The briefcase—it's got the group captain's initials on it!* He leaned over the rail and grabbed the briefcase and tossed the automatic pistol to where Woo's body lay, surrounded by the rapidly nearing flames. The fire would destroy my fingerprints on the weapon, he thought, as he descended the ladder.

'Away down river, as quick as you can, Joe! We don't want to be in the vicinity when the river police arrive to investigate the fire.' Saying this, Barry jumped into the speedboat.

Joe swung the wheel around and headed the motorboat away from the burning vessel and down towards the river's estuary. About a quarter of a mile away from the stricken cabin cruiser, they heard a muffled explosion. 'The fire must have got to the fuel tank,' said Joe.

'Now turn back up river on the other side and head back to the jetty,' said Barry.

Joe turned the boat, went in close to the bank and headed back to the jetty.

'You guys are really something else! I never thought of either of you as being "action men", but you sure carried that operation off like you do it for a living. And, Barry, that was pretty nifty shooting through the briefcase. He'd have shot you dead for sure if you hadn't got him first. I seem to recall a scene like that in an old black and white film of the forties.'

'Yes, Ruby, that's what gave me the idea. Humphrey Bogart, playing the Ernest Hemingway character, Harry Morgan, did it in *To Have and Have Not*, when he pretended to get a match from his desk, where he kept his gun, and shot a Vichy French gunman through the desktop.'

'But tell me, Barry, why did you shoot the other gunman? You had the drop on him and could have taken him prisoner.'

'The man's clothes were on fire and he would have probably been burnt alive. So I thought it an act of mercy to prevent his unnecessary suffering. Anyway, he would have shot me if I had hesitated and you and Joe, who was unarmed, would have been his next victims.'

Ruby looked thoughtful for a few seconds. 'I'm sorry, Barry, I didn't see it like that at the time. But I can now understand that you had little choice in the matter. Thank you for saving my life.'

Barry smiled down at her and took her hand in his. 'Think nothing of it, Ruby, it was a real pleasure to do so.'

As Joe brought the speedboat alongside the jetty's end, Barry looked across to the river and saw that two police launches were moored alongside the trees where the cabin cruiser had been anchored. The fire on the cabin cruiser had been extinguished and the police were carefully examining the burnt out hulk.

Joe secured the speedboat to the jetty rail and called the boat owner. The owner approached and looked at Ruby, questioningly.

'We went to collect this lady from a ship down at estuary,' explained Barry. 'What's been going on across the river?' asked Barry, as an interested tourist might do.

The boat owner scratched his head. 'I hear one bang, like gun. I look out my hut and see fire on big boat. A little later I hear very big bang, like explosion.'

'Did you see any other boats near the big boat at same time?' asked Barry, trying to keep his questioning simple.

'No, only boats passing up and down middle of river.'

Barry smiled benevolently at the boat owner. 'We've really enjoyed our time in your boat. Here's a bonus for you, a bit extra for having another passenger,' Barry said, handing the man a ten baht note.

Back in the Landrover, Ruby rearranged her tousled hair. 'I must look a real mess,' she said.

'Not at all,' replied Barry. 'If you don't mind me saying, I think you look terrific. But I expect you'd like to have a shower and make use of your make-up kit.'

'Thank you for your kind words, Barry; flattery it may be, but it does my morale a power of good to hear them after what I've been through. I certainly could do with a shower and change of clothing, so would you take me back to the Oriental Hotel?'

'I don't think that would be wise for you to go back there yet. Woo's men know you are staying there and we don't know if any of them are still hanging about the hotel.'

'But I need some personal things and a change of clothing.'

'OK, we'll compromise, I'll escort you up to your room to collect what you need and then we can go to our house. We have everything else there that you might need and we do have female servants to help you.'

'Yes, that sounds all right. I've been to a party at your house with Group Captain Tremayne. I'm sure I'll feel safe and comfortable there,' Ruby said with a smile.

'OK, Joe, let's go. Oriental first, for a few minutes and then back to our house.'

'Barry, you haven't forgotten, have you? The group captain wants us to meet him at 1900 hours at the airport and it's five o'clock now.'

'Yes, it had rather slipped my mind with everything else that has been happening. But we've got plenty of time for Ruby to get herself fixed up and then we can take her with us to meet the group captain. I'm sure he'll be delighted to see that she is safe and unharmed.'

CHAPTER 32

❀

As soon as Tremayne and Feng arrived back at Phnom Penh, Feng went straight to a telephone and rang Lloyd. 'Feng here,' he said to Lloyd's telephone operator.

'What is your codename?' asked the operator.

'Henry Kissinger,' replied Feng.

Lloyd came on the line. 'What have you to report, Feng?'

'The cargo was delivered as planned and I have the payment, in US Dollars, with me.'

'Splendid, Feng, you have done well. I want you to now return to Bangkok with Tremayne and telephone me again as soon as you get there. Then go to your hotel and stay there, guarding the money with your life.'

'Yes, Mr Lloyd I—'

But Lloyd had hung up.

Feng joined Tremayne and the others at the aircraft.

'Mr Lloyd wants us to return to Bangkok and await instructions.'

'What did he say about releasing my son?' Rantzen asked.

'Yes, and what about Miss Carterton?' added Tremayne. 'Has he told Woo to release her?'

'He said nothing about them. He will probably contact Woo in the meantime and tell him to release your woman, Group Captain Tremayne.'

'But what about my son?' said Rantzen, his anger rising.

'I don't know what Lloyd's plans are to release your son. I imagine he will send him down to Bangkok to join you on the next available flight. You will just have to wait and see. Now, can we get back to Bangkok, Group Captain?'

The flight back to Bangkok was uneventful and Tremayne touched down a few minutes before the planned ETA. He taxied the aircraft to its usual parking space and after locking the cabin led his companions to the arrivals lounge.

Tremayne, Rantzen and Mellors ordered coffee and brandy and Feng went straight to a telephone booth to phone Lloyd.

Lloyd was seated, waiting by the phone for Feng's call. No code name was asked for when Feng came on the line, but he preambled his speech with "Henry Kissinger here".

Before Feng could say another word, Lloyd shouted down the line: 'The whole operation's gone sour! Those Viet Cong idiots who collected our freight at the border got themselves ambushed by South Vietnamese troops a couple of miles down the road. Five of them were either killed or captured and the goods were impounded. The only survivor managed to hide and got away later to phone me here. He said that someone must have tipped off the South Vietnamese troops and that his boss expects us to produce another load, or return the money. I want that money; I have plans for its use. So another load will have to be prepared for transportation by the same method.'

'Mr Lloyd, wouldn't it be better to just keep the money and forget about trying to get another consignment to them?' suggested Feng.

'No, it wouldn't, you fool. We'd have Pathet Lao troops all over us if we tried to double-cross the Viet Cong. I want you to tell Tremayne that I want him up here early tomorrow morning to pick up another load.'

'Tremayne's not going to like that. He wasn't expecting to do more than one flight, and he and his crew will be very tired after today.'

'Never mind all that Feng, just do as I say. If Tremayne gives you an argument remind him we still hold the hostages and if he wants them back alive, he's to do as I tell him.'

'Very well, Mr Lloyd, I shall do as you command, but I have a strange feeling that things will not go as you would want this time and—'

But Lloyd had replaced his receiver.

Feng stepped out of the telephone booth and was standing outside the arrival lounge lighting a cigarette when Joe drove the to the entrance of the arrivals lounge.

He gaped in horror when he saw Barry helping Ruby down from the Landrover.

Tremayne looked up at the window when he heard the Landrover pulling up at the door and saw Barry, Joe *and Ruby*, get out of the vehicle, watched by Feng. 'Quick, Mellors, grab that Laotian bandit—before he gets back on the phone to Lloyd!'

Tremayne, Rantzen and Mellors rushed out of the office. Mellors grabbed Feng before he could produce his pistol, grasped him in a tight headlock and disarmed him.

Tremayne rushed over to Ruby and, ignoring the audience, clasped her to him. 'Darling, thank God you're safe. I've suffered a thousand agonies fearing what might be happening to you.'

Ruby released herself from his hold. 'I'm unharmed, Randy, thanks to your two heroes. They were magnificent. But let's all go in the lounge and have a stiff drink and I'll tell you everything that has happened to me while you've been away.'

Rantzen ordered drinks for everyone. Feng sat morose-faced, guarded by Mellors, and Ruby narrated her story. When she had finished, Tremayne looked admiringly at Barry and Joe. 'If this had been an *official operation*, I would cite you both for an award. But as it wasn't you'll just have to be satisfied with my everlasting gratitude. But tell me, Barry, what did you do with the briefcase and pistol?'

'I threw the pistol down beside Woo. The fire will have destroyed my fingerprints. I kept the briefcase; it's in the Landrover. I didn't think it would be wise to leave it at the scene with your initials on it, in case it wasn't completely destroyed by the fire. I'm afraid it's got a rather nasty hole in it, so you'll have to watch your brandy flask doesn't fall through it.'

Everyone laughed, except Feng.

'As it happens, Barry, I took that gun from one of Woo's men and think it is quite likely to have been registered to Woo. So, after checking the serial number of the gun, the police will probably satisfy themselves that an enemy, such as a desperate punter, who was deeply in debt to him, had sent the two Laotian gunmen to kill or rob Woo, and that they had all been killed in an exchange of gunfire. And a stray bullet had hit the petrol tank and caused the explosion and fire.'

'Well, Randy, your guys certainly came up trumps in rescuing Miss Carterton; but what about Ben? Lloyd's still got him up in Laos.'

'Yes, Brad, I've not forgotten about Ben. I think we'd all better get back to my house and hold a council of war to decide what we are going to do about getting him freed. But first, what do you want to do, Ruby—go to another hotel, or stay at my house?'

Ruby thought for a moment. 'I think I better book into another hotel. I've heard the Erawan Hotel is very good. I'll have the Oriental Hotel housemaid pack up my things and bring them over there when I'm booked in. You can drop me off at the Erawan when you and the others leave for your house. I must telephone my father; he will have been trying to reach me during the last two days and if I don't get in touch with him soon he'll probably get on to the embassy to get the police to make enquiries.'

'Very well, Ruby, if that's what you want, we'll do that,' said Tremayne, trying not to look disappointed in front of the others. 'Yes, you'd better ring your father; the last thing we want is for the Thai police to start looking into your *disappearance.*'

'Group Captain Tremayne, I have something to say to you. Something that might have a great bearing on what you plan to do next,' said Feng.

Everyone turned to look at Feng.

'Well, Feng, what have you to say?'

'Mr Lloyd instructed me to tell you that the South Vietnamese Army captured the last consignment of freight. This consignment was paid for and Mr Lloyd, being a man of honour, wishes to deliver a replacement consignment to our Viet Cong customers. He instructed me to tell you that you are to fly up to Vientiane tomorrow morning to collect this consignment and deliver it via Phnom Penh to our customers.'

Sergeant Mellors nearly exploded with rage. 'You're not delivering shit to the Commie bastards. Doing that is tantamount to treason!'

'That's enough from you, Carl! Group Captain Tremayne is doing what he is doing to save my son,' said Rantzen reproachfully.

'It's OK, Brad, I can understand Sergeant Mellors' feelings in the matter. Especially when there is a strong likelihood that drugs supplied to the Viet Cong are intended for distribution to peddlers to sell, or even give away, to your troops and other SEATO members' forces in the field. Let's leave the matter until we get back to my house. But before we go I want to put Feng straight about his position.'

Trermayne turned to face Feng. 'You're finished, Feng, as good as dead. We have the money the Viet Cong entrusted to you, locked in the Devon's baggage section, and without that Lloyd will never accept you back. My guess is that he will probably send men after you to recover the money, and kill you if you don't hand it over. You would be well advised to consider throwing in your lot with us. If you agree, and do as I say, we might let you live and even give you some of Lloyd's money to help you to get away.'

Feng inwardly digested what he had heard. It made sense. If he didn't go along with what this mad British officer wanted, he would probably kill him. Lloyd certainly *would* if he returned without his money. He nodded. 'Just tell me what I am to do.'

'Later, Feng, when we reach my home. Now, let's be off. Ruby, you and Colonel Rantzen in my car; Barry, you take Joe, Sergeant Mellors and Feng in the Landrover and we'll meet at my house.'

Back at the house, Tremayne got Sutep to make a pile of sandwiches and a large pot of coffee. They all sat around Tremayne's large dining table and ate sandwiches and drank coffee while they listened to Tremayne's plan of action. When he had finished talking he brought out his arsenal of weapons: the two carbines, the Nambu automatic and Feng's automatic pistol and spare clips, the sword stick, the stiletto and all the spare magazines for the weapons. 'Brad and Carl. you take the carbines and spare mags and the stiletto. I'll have the Nambu automatic, Feng's pistol and the swordstick.'

'What about Joe and me?' Barry asked.

Tremayne looked hard at Barry. 'I want you and Joe to be our rearguard and to look after Miss Carterton. And, if necessary, answer questions put to you by any inquisitive need-to-know people at the embassy. Tell them I'm on a secret intelligence-gathering trip up in Laos, and expect to be back tomorrow.' Turning to Joe: 'I want everything checked out for a 0600 hours flight tomorrow. Make sure our tanks, including the auxiliary one, are filled to capacity; I don't want to have to refuel at Vientiane. Tell the Air

Traffic Control people that the timings will be exactly as they were yesterday, and I'll put it all in writing when I get to the airport. Oh, just one other thing, Joe, we've got three or four parachutes in our airport store. Turn them out and put them on the Devon. Now, I suggest that we all get some sleep. Brad, you and Carl can stay here and sleep on the sofas if you want to. Barry and Joe, you'll want to get back to your house. You'll need the Landrover to get to the airport in the morning, Joe. Samarn will take us in the car to the airport and bring it back here. Any questions?'

'What do we do with Feng, sir?' asked Mellors.

'Tie him to one of those chairs. Not too tightly, though. I want him to be able to drive tomorrow,' said Tremayne.

'Randy, there's no need to worry about him getting free in the night without being heard. I wake at the sound of a feather falling,' said Rantzen, loud enough for Feng to hear.

'Feng's got too much to lose by leaving us. We have Lloyd's money and he daren't return to Vientiane, and now that Woo's been eliminated he's got no friends in Bangkok. Now let's get some shuteye,' said Tremayne, stretching out on a sofa.

Rantzen and Mellors followed suit and soon the only sound in the room was gentle snoring from the four men.

CHAPTER 33

❀

'Ready for takeoff, Brad?' asked Tremayne as he fired the Devon's twin engines.

'Sure as eggs is eggs, skipper,' answered Rantzen above the roar of the engines.

'Then we are off!' shouted Tremayne as he accelerated the Devon down the runway at takeoff speed.

Brad felt rejuvenated—better than he had done for years. He was going into action again—a time when he felt he was at his best. He wasn't meant to be shuffling paper, making small talk at embassy cocktail parties, or stooging for superiors like Colonel Merkle. He'd experienced more action in an afternoon in Korea than Merkle might get in a lifetime in the service. Merkle wasn't a true warrior; he was half a politician, always looking for the main chance to enhance his prospects. He was a born boot licker, and almost a one-star general who would never know what it was like to lead a formation of fighter planes in a real air battle.

Carl Mellors, seated in the passengers' cabin, was thinking about how he had got into the present situation. Lieutenant Colonel Rantzen, the only officer he had ever respected and even liked, had asked him if he'd help him out in an unofficial operation to rescue his son from the Communists. He'd agreed and had no regrets. Hadn't the colonel gone to bat for him in getting him educated enough to be accepted for aircrew training—thereby saving him from a life of menial servitude for a bunch of "better than thou" officers who had to have help to press their pants? And, anyway, he'd always wanted to have a crack at the Commies, but being radio operator didn't afford a man much chance of getting into a personal shooting war with your enemies. So, going after some drug peddling sons-of-bitches who wanted to get the US Army hopped up with drugs, was a bonus reason for helping his colonel. Carl Mellors now saw himself with the vanguard of a crusade, to save the freedom loving peoples of the democratic countries of the world from Communism.

Feng, smoking cigarettes that Carl Mellors had given him, felt full of hope for the future. He thought of how easily one's fortune could change. Two days ago he would have killed any of his present companions without a qualm and they would probably have killed him. Now, it seemed, they were his saviours—giving him a chance of a new life, within the law and with money to help him settle in a new country. He thought he'd like to settle somewhere in the Americas. Almost everyone was welcome there if they had money and were without a criminal record. This made him smile when he thought of the crimes he had committed and yet had never come to the notice of any police force.

Tremayne was concentrating on his airmanship. He'd promised to help Rantzen get his son back and that's what he'd do. But thoughts of Ruby kept entering this mind. She'd seemed different when they had met at the airport, even a bit off-hand with him. But to be fair, she'd had a nasty experience. It had probably been worse at the hands of Woo than she had let on. He'd have to spoil her a bit when he got back. She'd soon come around.

A half-hour before touchdown Tremayne rang the embassy in Vientiane and asked that a large four-wheel drive vehicle be left at the airport for his use. 'I need something pretty rugged, I'm off up country again,' he had explained to the transport manager. 'But I won't need one of your drivers. The man I've got is very familiar with the area I'm visiting.'

Tremayne landed the Devon and taxied it to his designated parking site. The embassy driver had arrived to see the Devon land and drove the long-based Landrover over to where the Devon was parked.

Rantzen and Mellors unloaded the weapons wrapped in hessian sacks and stowed them behind the rear seats of the Landrover.

'Are you not taking the money with you, Group Captain Tremayne?' asked Feng.

'No, Feng, it'll be quite safe in the aircraft until we return, and when we get back I'll give you the money I promised you—20, 000 US dollars! But you'll earn it and if you don't do exactly as I say when we get to Lloyd's place, you'll not get a red cent,' snapped Tremayne.

Feng grinned broadly. 'For 20,000 US dollars, Group Captain, I'd murder my mother!'

'We'll not be murdering any mothers today, Feng, but I'm glad you know what is expected of you. Now give the embassy driver a tip and enough for taxi fare and tell him to make his way back to the embassy. Tell him we've no idea when we shall return, but when we do the vehicle will be left here for his collection.'

Tremayne secured the aircraft and the four men boarded the Landrover. Feng was in the driving seat with Tremayne sat next to him. Tremayne lent the swordstick against the dashboard, put Feng's pistol on the seat at his right side and put the Nambu pistol in the left-hand pocket of his bush shirt. He put the spare clips for the pistols in the breast pockets of his shirt. Rantzen and Mellors sat in the rear seats, with the hessian wrapped carbines and spare magazines under their seats.

'Off you go then, Feng. Not too fast, keep within the speed limits; I don't want us to be stopped by a Lao policeman who doesn't know what CD plates mean,' said Tremayne.

Feng drove slowly away from the airport and headed up the now familiar route to Lloyd's drug production centre.

No one spoke, just sat with grim determined expressions on their faces.

Tremayne broke the silence. 'I estimate we are about ten miles from Lloyd's place,' said Tremayne, turning to Feng.

Feng nodded agreement.

'Now is the time for us to check our weapons and make them ready for instant use,' said Tremayne.

Rantzen and Mellors took out the carbines, worked their actions and fitted magazines.

Tremayne turned in his seat to face Rantzen and Mellors. 'When we get to the gate, Feng will be recognised by the guards and they will open the gate. Feng will drive right up to the front door of Lloyd's house. With a bit of luck Lloyd will come to the door to meet Feng and me. You two keep well out of sight but ready for instant action. No shooting until I shout the order, or you come under fire from Lloyd's men. I want Lloyd alive, as our hostage, until we reach Ben. With a bit of luck we may be able to get to Ben without firing a shot, but if we don't have Lloyd under our control all hell will break loose. There must be at least fifty men working in this drug factory; I saw at least a dozen men armed with automatic weapons, and there are two Dobermans, with handlers, patrolling the wire. If a firefight breaks out don't move too far away from the vehicle. We'll certainly need to make a quick getaway. I didn't see any vehicles in the compound, but I'm sure they do have some, and Lloyd's men might well give chase.'

'Yes,' said Feng, 'they have three Landrovers and a light van, parked behind the processing sheds. But there is one very important thing you have overlooked, Group Captain. When Lloyd meets us at his door he will expect me to be carrying a large sack of US dollars. If I have no money to give him he will be very suspicious and call on his men to seize us both.'

Tremayne cursed himself for not having thought of that. 'Right, we'll have to make up a parcel to look like a large bag of money. Brad, let me have those sacks you wrapped the weapons in. Sergeant, lift out those seat cushions and put them in these sacks.' Tremayne passed the sacks to Mellors. The leather seat cushions fitted into the sacks and could reasonably be thought to contain two large packages of currency. Tremayne held them up for Feng's inspection. 'Wouldn't you agree that these look very much like the package you picked up at the Cambodian border, the sort of thing that Lloyd would expect?'

'Yes, they look just like the real thing, but you'll have to get the drop on Lloyd before he looks inside those sacks,' said Feng.

'Let me worry about that one. We'll carry a sack each in front of us when we get out of the vehicle.'

Feng smiled. 'That is a good idea, to hide your pistol behind the bag. Woo told me how you tricked him with your gun in bag act. We are almost there now, Group Captain.'

'Get under cover, you two,' ordered Tremayne.

Feng drove slowly up to the gate and shouted a greeting to the two guards as they swung open the gates. Tremayne noted there were several armed men patrolling the wired compound. Feng drove up to the steps leading to Lloyd's front door. Tremayne and Feng got out of the vehicle carrying the two sacks in front of them. Tremayne held his in his left hand and his right hand grasped the Nambu automatic in his bush jacket pocket.

Lloyd appeared at the front door. 'Ah, Group Captain Tremayne, I'm so pleased you agreed to continue in my service! And Feng, I see you have the money. Too much for you to carry, was it?

A good thing you had some assistance. Count yourself lucky; RAF group captains are not accustomed to being used as baggage handlers. Please bring the bags into my house.'

Lloyd led the way into the hallway. As soon as he and Feng were out of sight of the outside guards, Tremayne drew his pistol and rammed it into Lloyd's back. 'Call for your men and you're dead,' said Tremayne with quiet malice.

'I've no wish to die, but tell me, Tremayne, how do you think that you, alone, could possibly shoot your way out of my stronghold with one little pistol? And haven't you forgotten the man by your side is mine, and he is armed and at the first opportunity will turn the tables on you?' Lloyd almost whispered.

'Sorry to disappoint you, but he's changed sides, Lloyd, and there's no money in these sacks. Now take me to where you are holding Ben Rantzen, or I'll take great delight in blowing a great big hole in the back of your shiny white head,' whispered Tremayne.

Lloyd spread his arms in a sign of surrender. 'It seems that you have the advantage for the moment. Follow me and you shall have your lieutenant.'

They slowly walked down the long winding passageway until they reached the door with the man sitting outside nursing a sub-machine gun. He placed his weapon against the wall and rose as Lloyd approached.

Lloyd rapped three times on the door and it was opened by one of Ben's guards. As Tremayne moved his pistol from Lloyd's back to cover the two guards, Lloyd pushed him aside and ran back down the corridor, shouting to his men. Feng snatched up the sub-machine gun from the floor and shot the guard at the door. Before the guard who had opened the door could draw his gun, Tremayne rammed his pistol into his gut and pushed him backwards into the room. The other guard was on his feet with his gun in his hand. He fired at what he could see of Tremayne, but hit his fellow guard in the back of his head. Blood and brains spurted over Tremayne as he fired back twice. The man dropped to the floor with two neat holes in his forehead and his blood, brains and bits of bone splattered against the wall behind him.

Ben was as Tremayne had last seen him—his legs manacled together and his left arm chained to the arm of the chair. 'Where are the keys, Ben?'

'In his pocket,' said Ben, pointing to the man Tremayne had shot.

Feng quickly found the keys and tossed them to Ben.

The sound of automatic gunfire and the *crack-crack* single shots of the M1 carbines could be heard from outside. Tremayne handed the Nambu automatic and spare clip to Ben. 'There's only two rounds left in that; better reload with the full clip while you have a chance.'

Tremayne picked up the two pistols dropped by the guards and put them in his pockets.

'Is there another way out of here?' asked Tremayne. 'They'll have the front door covered and we'll be sitting ducks for them as we run out.'

'Yes, there is a side door, which will bring us around the back of the process shed and behind the men who are at the front of the building.'

'Good, then let's go!' shouted Tremayne.

Feng led the way and unlocked the side door with a short burst of the sub-machine gun.

They ran to the back of the processing building. The shooting had now lessened to sporadic individual shots and short bursts of automatic fire.

Tremayne saw the parked line of vehicles. 'Will the keys be with them?'

Feng nodded and pointed to one of the Landrovers. 'Take this one; it is Lloyd's personal vehicle. It is armoured plated, has bullet-proof glass and self-sealing tyres.'

The three men climbed in. 'Feng, give your gun to Ben, and Ben, you take the right side and I'll cover the left. Now, Feng, drive like the clappers to the main gate.'

The vehicle shot forward and headed straight at the gate. As they approached Tremayne could see Rantzen and Mellors crouched against the side of the embassy Landrover. Nine or ten bodies and two Dobermans lay dead in the area, but no sign of Lloyd.

'Smash the gate down, Feng, and then stop to pick up the others. Ben, cover your father and Mellors as they get aboard this vehicle. Here, you must be nearly out of ammo, take these two pistols.'

Feng crashed into the gate and knocked it flat and stopped. Rantzen and Mellors got the message. The embassy Landrover was shot full of holes and its tyres were flat. It had made its last journey.

Rantzen and Mellors, both slightly wounded, ran from their cover to board Lloyd's vehicle. Several of Lloyd's men came out of their cover to fire at them.

'Quick, get aboard, Colonel, I'll cover you,' said Mellors, turning to fire back at the pursuing Laotians.

Rantzen scrambled to the door of the Landrover and was pulled in by Ben. Mellors emptied his carbine at the advancing Laotian gunmen. Four of their number fell dead or wounded, but the remainder followed Mellors, firing as they went. As Mellors reached the vehicle he was hit in the back by a stream of bullets. Ben returned fire and downed two more of the Laotians.

'Ben, get Mellors into the vehicle!' cried Rantzen. 'I'll cover you.'

'Too late, Dad, he's dead.'

'Drive back to those other vehicles, Feng!' shouted Tremayne. 'Brad, Ben, aim at the van's petrol tank and the Landrovers' tyres as we drive by.'

Rantzen and Ben's fusillade of shots hit their target and the van's petrol tank exploded—the flames spreading to the other vehicles until they were all ablaze.

'Feng, now drive us out of here as fast as this thing will take us.'

As they drove through the gate, more of Lloyd's men reappeared from where they had been sheltering from Rantzen's and Mellors' deadly accurate shooting, and blazed away, without effect, at the armoured vehicle.

Several miles south of Lloyd's complex, Tremayne ordered Feng to stop. Then turned to face Rantzen on the back seat. 'Let's have a look at that wound of yours.'

'It's nothing, Randy, just a nick in the shoulder, I'll be OK. I've got Mellors to thank for my life.'

Brad and Ben talked almost non-stop and Feng kept his eyes on the road and drove slower as they approached the suburbs of the city. Tremayne thought about the possible consequences of what had been happening during the last few days. If it all came to light he'd have a lot to explain and not much of it would favour him. Whatever happened he would make sure Barry and Joe were not implicated. They'd made the whole operation possible by rescuing Ruby and that was something he wouldn't forget.

Arriving at the airport, Feng went to a pharmacy and bought some dressings for Rantzen. Ben dressed his father's wound in the public washrooms.

Tremayne telephoned the Erawan, but Ruby was not in her room, so he left a message to say he had got back to Vientiane and he would see her as soon as he could, after he had landed at Don Muang.

Rantzen and Ben went in to arrivals lounge and ordered steaks and beer.

Tremayne called Feng to join him in the Devon, where he opened the baggage lockup and took out the huge sack of money. He split open a large packet of notes and counted out two hundred 100-dollar bills, while Feng looked on, his eyes gleaming.

'There you are, Feng, 20,000 US dollars, just what I promised you—you've earned it,' said Tremayne, handing him the wad of notes.

Feng peeled off the top note and riffled it in his hand, then held it up to the light. 'This is a counterfeit bill!' He checked another and another. 'They are all counterfeit notes,' he said with a sob in his voice. He passed one to Tremayne to check.

Tremayne examined the note. 'It looks OK to me! What's wrong with it? How do you know it's a counterfeit note?'

Feng laughed hysterically. 'Because, my friend, every bill has the same serial number!'

'Which only goes to prove that, as has so long been believed, there is no honour among thieves,' said Tremayne.

Feng dropped the wad of notes on the floor. 'Millions of dollars, but the only value they have is to be used in that capitalistic game called *Monopoly* you westerners play!'

Tremayne couldn't resist a silent chuckle at Feng's unintentional humour. 'Hold on Feng, you could still use them. The only thing you'd have to watch is that you didn't spend more than one note at any one shop or restaurant. You could move around the world spending single hundred dollar bills everywhere.'

'No, Tremayne, I could not spend this money without taking a very high risk of them being quickly identified as counterfeit. Without consecutive numbering, it is obvious that they are very amateurishly forged notes, and they will have many other faults that could easily be spotted by shopkeepers and bank clerks. What you have to understand is that, in the Far East, the presentation of a US 100-dollar bill always raises eyebrows, if not suspicion.'

'So, what do you want to do, Feng, stay in Vientiane or come back with us to Bangkok?'

'I think I should like to go to Bangkok. There is much pleasure to be had in that city and I intend to stay there enjoying it until I'm caught spending this fake currency,' said Feng, picking up a handful of the bills from the floor.

'Come on then, we'll join the others for a meal and a drink before we take off for Bangkok,' said Tremayne, but his priority was telephoning the Erawan Hotel again to see if Ruby had returned from wherever she had been.

Rantzen and Ben had almost finished their meal and were raring to get back to Bangkok, so Tremayne had his brandy flask filled and ordered sandwiches for himself and Feng. He paid—he didn't want to take the risk of Feng being caught passing counterfeit currency while he was in his company. He thought it wiser not to tell the others about the counterfeit dollars until they were back in Bangkok.

Before boarding the Devon, Tremayne telephoned Ruby's hotel. She was still out and hadn't been seen all day. This was worrying; where could she be out on her own for so long? Maybe she wasn't on her own. Tremayne began to think that perhaps it hadn't been a good idea to ask Barry to look after Ruby. He was about the same age as Ruby, polite, personable, with a good physique and a veneer of sophistication that was probably quite attractive to women who admired such qualities. Then he dismissed the whole idea. Barry Marshall was just a flight sergeant in the RAF and Ruby was a wealthy socialite in Australia and could have the pick of men of education, power and wealth. He counted himself lucky to have been able to seduce and court her to the point where she had accepted him as her lover and potential lifetime partner.

Back on the Devon, with Tremayne and Rantzen at the controls and Ben yarning with Feng in the passenger cabin, there was an atmosphere of restrained camaraderie. The subject foremost in all their minds was the death of Mellors. Rantzen knew that he would have some difficult questions to answer about the death of the USAF crewman. Ben had not known Mellors personally, but he was deeply moved by the sergeant's sacrifice, which had not only helped to save his life, but also that of his father.

Tremayne had known Sergeant Mellors only very slightly, but was regretful, and said as much to Rantzen. 'You had a good man there, Brad. It's a long time since I'd seen such loyalty shown by a man to his commanding officer. And he deserves a medal for bravery in the face of an enemy. But I imagine that it would be difficult for you to do anything about that.'

'Yes, I'm afraid that if all this comes out I should almost certainly face a General Court Martial, which would doubtless result at the very least in me losing my commission and being cashiered from the service, without a pension.'

Even Feng added his homage. 'That Sergeant Mellors was a damned good soldier. He fought and died like a real hero.'

They were about half an hours flying time out of Vientiane when the port engine made a spluttering noise and went dead. The aircraft dipped sharply to port, throwing the passengers out of their seats. Tremayne wrestled with the controls to trim the aircraft, but it went further into descent.

'We'll not stay in he air with this one engine with the weight we've got aboard. The starboard engine has been acting up as well. The aircraft was due a second line servicing last month and with all the flying I've been doing lately both the power plants are unreliable,' said Tremayne with a trace of alarm in his voice.

'What'll we do to lighten the load, Randy? Throw out the passenger seats?'

'No, Brad, that will not make sufficient difference to keep us in the air. We've got to lessen the load on the starboard engine before we reach the point of no return.'

'Why not return to Vientiane now? We're not that far out.'

'No, there's a better way—some of us must bail out when we are over less mountainous country and near a town.'

'Bail out? I didn't think you carried chutes in the plane, Randy.'

'I asked Joe Swaine to put our chutes aboard before we left Bangkok. I'm sure we have at least two. How's your shoulder? Do you think you could make it without causing yourself any more damage?'

'Sure thing; I'm OK; I can make it.'

'Here's the key to the baggage store, Brad, the chutes are in there. Tell Ben to get a chute on and be ready to jump out as soon as we are near a safe dropping zone.'

'What about Feng?'

'If there are enough chutes to go round he can have one if he wants it, but I think you'll find that he might rather stay on board and take his chances. Oh, and by the way, that money in the store is worthless—all counterfeit. Feng spotted it.'

'Counterfeit dollars, where did they come from?' asked Rantzen.

'As far as I can gather, the North Vietnamese Army supplied them to their Viet Cong agents. The counterfeit notes probably originated in some Communist state, such as Red China, or the USSR. As you are aware, both those countries support North Vietnam's action in South Vietnam, and the proliferation of forged US dollars throughout the Far East could be damaging to the US economy.'

'So what are you going to do with them, Randy?'

'I haven't made up my mind yet. Probably paper the rooms in my house with them,' said Tremayne with a forced laugh. 'Anyway, time to saddle up, we're almost over Phetchburi, an ideal spot to drop onto.'

Rantzen went into the passenger cabin, opened the store and found that there were three parachutes. He told Ben and Feng what they had to do. 'It's the skipper's orders. He says he can't guarantee to keep this kite airborne with so many heavyweights aboard.'

Ben had no parachuting experience, but Rantzen quickly explained the technique. 'What we must do is drop as a "stick" and keep together. If we do that we'll not end up too far apart when we hit the ground.'

'I've got her down to the right height for you to jump. Open the door, Brad, and when I shout "go", jump at three-second intervals. Good luck and safe landings to you all! I'll see you at the Erawan Hotel for a celebratory drink tomorrow!' Tremayne shouted through the open flight deck door.

Rantzen arranged the jump order: Ben, Feng and himself last.

'Go now!' roared Tremayne.

'So-long, and thanks a million, sir, I look forward to buying you that drink!' shouted Ben over his shoulder as he jumped through the door.

'Goodbye, Group Captain Tremayne, I hope to see you one day in Bangkok, but I think I will soon be in prison!' shouted Feng as he threw himself out of the plane.

Rantzen entered the flight deck and sat in the vacant seat.

'What in hell's name are you doing, Brad? You should have jumped with the others.'

'You forgot something, Randy; someone had to close the door. And, anyway, if you are going to land this crippled kite, you'll need all the help you can get.'

'Yes, you're right Brad, but keep that chute handy in case the other engine fails.'

'If that happens, Randy, you must take the chute. You've put yourself on the line for my boy.'

'We'll see,' replied Tremayne, as he fiddled with switches. Suddenly the port engine spluttered and came alive. Tremayne levelled the aircraft and made a 180-degree turn.

'What happened there? That engine sounds healthy enough to me!' Rantzen gasped incredulously.

Tremayne laughed. 'Yes, it is, and I turned the aeroplane around so that we could fly back to Vientiane, to return the money to Mr George Lloyd.'

'Why bother with that, it's all useless counterfeit.'

Tremayne laughed. 'I know, that's the whole point of the exercise; I wouldn't give it to him if it were any good. I just want to cause him bitter disappointment.'

'Oh, I get it! I'm all for that, Randy.'

Tremayne pulled his brandy flask out of his hip pocket and offered it to Rantzen. 'Fill the cap for yourself and pass the flask back to me. We'll have a little drink to while away the time until we get to Vientiane.'

And so it was that the two, now tarnished heroes, drank brandy and exchanged macabre jokes, as Tremayne hurled the Devon at maximum speed towards Vientiane.

'There's Vientiane below us now,' said Tremayne, before taking a final swig from his flask.

Rantzen looked out of the window, at the millions of twinkling lights. 'It looks pretty at night, but it's not so pretty in the daytime.'

'Yes, Brad, you're absolutely right—there is no doubt; cities always seem to look better at night. We've not far to go now, so perhaps you'd like to unpack that money. Break all the seals and stack it by the door ready to hand over to Mr Lloyd.'

Rantzen eagerly left his seat like a young boy going to his first football match.

Tremayne started a slow descent of the Devon. Down to five hundred feet and the buildings of George Lloyd's drug producing empire were now made visible by his perimeter lights. He made a low pass over Lloyd's house. All the internal lights suddenly came on and men, some with weapons, came running out of the outbuildings. Tremayne made another low pass at rooftop height. Some of the men started shooting up at the Devon and several bullets tore through its fuselage.

'George Lloyd is now on top of his steps, Brad. Open the door and throw out the money!' shouted Tremayne above the sound of the aircraft's engines and the now heavy gunfire.

As the Devon again passed low over the buildings, Rantzen laughed and jeered through the open door at the men below and hurled handfuls of 100-dollar bills over the buildings. Most of the men stopped firing and stooped to pick up the bills. Tremayne and Rantzen could see Lloyd screaming orders at his men to gather up the money as it floated to earth. Soon thirty or forty of Lloyd's men were busy picking up the money. Lloyd came down from his steps and joined them, frantically picking up the bills before the light evening breeze and slipstream of the aircraft blew the money away.

'The money's all gone,' croaked Rantzen as he staggered back onto the flight deck, blood pouring from several bullet wounds in his chest. 'I've been hit bad, Randy. I guess I won't be joining you for that drink at the—.'

Tremayne turned to look at Rantzen and saw him slump back in his seat, give a gentle cough as blood poured from his mouth, and die.

'Right, you bastards, you've killed two good men today and now you'll pay!' screamed Tremayne as he put the Devon into a steep dive and flew it straight at the front of Lloyd's house.

Epilogue

❀

The massed congregation of British and American diplomats and their staffs and families, stood in silence as the Bangkok Christian chapel's organist played 'Lead, kindly light, amid the encircling gloom, lead thou me on...'

At the rear of the ranks of the Military Attaché Corps, stood Lieutenant Benjamin Rantzen, proud holder of the Silver Star, for gallantry in action, and an escaper from a Pathet Lao prison cage. He silently mouthed the words that followed, 'The night is dark and I am far from home,' as he thought of Group Captain Tremayne, Sergeant Mellors and his father, who had given their lives to save him, and were now ashes and dust lying amid the burnt-out ruins of a drug lord's empire in Laos.

His Excellency Sir Bertram Humphrey, Her Britannic Majesty's Ambassador to Thailand, rose to deliver his eulogy: 'Ladies and gentlemen, we are gathered here today to celebrate the life of a hero, Randolph Tremayne. He was a hero in every sense of the word, who bravely served his country in times of war. He was a loyal, dedicated, determined and resourceful officer who never spared himself in carrying out his duties an air attaché in the neighbouring war zones of the Far East. A few months ago he was returning alone in his twin-engine Devon aircraft, from a routine liaison visit to Vientiane, where he was the accredited air attaché. About 50 miles south of Vientiane his aircraft's port engine failed. In a final radio message to Bangkok air traffic control, he advised them that because he had doubts about the reliability of his starboard engine he intended to return to Vientiane and land there. Tragically, he never made it back to Vientiane and must have drifted off course—understandably, because he was not accompanied by his navigator, who had previously been admitted to hospital in Singapore—for it has been reported by the Laotian authorities that Group Captain Tremayne's aircraft crashed about 40 miles north-east of Vientiane, in an area, which is now under the control of Pathet Lao forces. His family, and his many friends and colleagues will, I am sure, sadly miss Group Captain Randolph Tremayne.'

The service over, Mrs Fiona Tremayne and her two children were standing at the chapel door to receive the condolences of the gathered assembly.

Barry Marshall approached the family. Over his shoulder, Mrs Tremayne could see Ruby Carterton standing outside near the chapel door.

'Mrs Tremayne, please accept my condolences for your tragic loss. Should you need any help in arranging for the handover of your house to the incoming air attaché, or the packing of your effects for conveyance to the UK, please don't hesitate to call on me.'

'Thank you Barry, it's very kind of you to offer your help, but everything has been arranged by Colonel Purvis and the First Secretary Administration.'

'Goodbye, Mrs Tremayne, Daphne, Peter,' said Barry, before he went to join Ruby Carterton outside the chapel.

'Goodbye, Barry,' said Mrs Tremayne, with a wry smile on her lips, as she watched Barry walk away, hand in hand, with Ruby Carterton.

The End

978-0-595-40750-7
0-595-40750-1